Sandy shoved past and out ⌐⎯⎯⎯⎯⎯⎯⎯⎯⎯ ran as if she were being chased, as fast as she coul⌐ past the back of the stables and down the farm drive towards its junction with the lane. She heard the hooves coming up the lane, still galloping, and ran till her heart nearly burst, but all she saw was the tail of the grey horse passing and the silver glint of its flying shoes. There was a slim boy bareback, leaning forward, with black hair flying, and no saddle, and only a rope for a rein: that much Sandy saw, but no more. The horse was gone and the thudding of its hooves receded into the silent autumn night.

There was a mist curling up slowly over the water-meadows and nothing moved again, only a heron kraaked from the reeds, and Sandy walked slowly home . . .

Also available by K.M. Peyton,
and published by Corgi Books

·THE BOY WHO WASN'T THERE·

For younger readers

POOR BADGER

THE WILD BOY
AND
QUEEN MOON

K.M.PEYTON

CORGI BOOKS

THE WILD BOY AND QUEEN MOON
A CORGI BOOK : 0 552 52750 5

First published in Great Britain by Doubleday,
a division of Transworld Publishers Ltd

PRINTING HISTORY
Doubleday edition published 1993
Corgi edition published 1995
Corgi edition reprinted 1995 (twice)

Copyright © 1993 by K.M. Peyton
Illustrations copyright © 1993 by Jon Riley
Cover illustration by Ann Carley

The right of K.M. Peyton to be identified as the author of
this work has been asserted in accordance with the
Copyright, Designs and Patents Act 1988

Corgi Books are published by Transworld Publishers Ltd,
61–63 Uxbridge Road, Ealing, London W5 5SA,
in Australia by Transworld Publishers (Australia) Pty Ltd,
15–25 Helles Avenue, Moorebank, NSW 2170,
and in New Zealand by Transworld Publishers (NZ) Ltd,
3 William Pickering Drive, Albany, Auckland.

Printed and bound in Great Britain by
Cox & Wyman Ltd, Reading, Berkshire

To Anna, Pip and Buster

Sandy made the fateful remark on the school bus when they were going home. It fell into one of those spasmodic silences that sometimes happen in a crowd, so that everyone heard.

'Any fool can win a hundred rosettes in a season when they've got a pony that cost twenty thousand pounds.'

The fool she was talking about, Julia Marsden, was sitting in the front seat and did not turn round. She felt as if a knife had sunk itself between her shoulder-blades.

Sandy went scarlet and hid her head in her voluminous duffle bag, scrambling for a book. Her friend Leo, beside her, whispered, 'That's a bit miaouwy for you,' and Sandy's brother Ian, sitting next to Julia, said to Julia kindly, 'Don't take any notice. It's sour grapes. Her pony's never won a rosette in its life.'

Then the hubbub started up again and everyone forgot the moment's awkwardness. Save Julia. And Sandy.

★　　★　　★

Last off the bus, far out in the country, Ian and Sandy got off at their lane end and dawdled home. The fields on either side were striped gold with stubble, basking in the early-evening, harvest-rich sun which was low over the ridge behind them. A small white sail drifted on the river below, beyond the marsh fields where the heifers were grazing. It was awful going back to school when the weather was still so good.

Sandy was an outdoor girl. She was gold and brown like the fields, her hair sun-bleached like the outside of a haybale; she was tough and stocky like a boy. When her hair was short she was taken for a boy. Yet her brother Ian, three years older, was willowy like a girl, wiry and hard and clever and not given to the outdoors. He scowled a lot, tied to a farm ten miles from his urban friends and interests.

'You shouldn't have said that,' he said. 'She can't help it.'

'I didn't mean anyone to hear, only Leo! It was awful. I could've died!'

'It's not her fault.'

'I know that! Honestly. I feel really mean.'

'She's got terrible parents.'

'Don't go *on*!'

Sandy's evening was blighted. She didn't like Julia, but she was sorry for her. Julia's parents were very ambitious and had bought her a top

JA pony which nearly always won, but also bit and kicked, bucked and bolted. Julia had a very hard life. She had a bad temper like her pony and was fast losing her nerve. Sandy knew that Julia did not deserve any more unkindnesses than she had to bear already.

Guilt lay heavily.

She sighed as they came down the slope to the dishevelled cottage where Flirtie Gertie lived.

'I'll call,' she said. 'Be nice to her.'

It might assuage the guilt. Usually they slipped past quietly, hoping the old woman wouldn't see them and waylay them with her batty remarks. Flirty Gertie was eighty-one, the widow of their grandfather's cowman, still living in the tied cottage, and their mother sent her up meals and kept a neighbourly eye on her. Their mother expected them to chat her up when they passed by – 'Sometimes she sees nobody all day!' – but they hated it. The old lady was no sweetie, but acerbic and smelly. She still hopped about like a mangy sparrow, sweeping and dusting and digging her potato bed, but her conversation wasn't very interesting.

'Tell your da the water's coming through the dormer window at the back – I've got to keep a bucket under it. And will you get me some elastic from the shop when you're up there next? Me knickers keep falling down. I've no fat left on me backside any longer, that's the real trouble.'

9

Ian had gone on, grinning, and Sandy stayed just long enough to feel good about it. The old girl wasn't bad; sometimes she laughed, but mostly it was complaints. She had a face as brown and wrinkled as a walnut, and black beady eyes which missed very little. Her wrists and ankles were thin as sticks and she wore old-fashioned brown stockings which wrinkled over her shoes, and a cross-over pinafore with tapes behind. She had wispy hair through which her skull showed through, none too cleanly.

'She's awful,' they complained to their mother.

'Yes, it's called old age,' their mother said cheerfully. 'We're all moving towards it, even you.'

Grandpa called her Flirty Gertie because when she was young she 'was a great one for the lads. She were a real pretty little thing.' Sandy couldn't think that far back. It was beyond her powers to see Gertie as a pretty little thing. The most awful thing she could think of was being really old. Yet neither Gertie nor Grandpa seemed to actually realize they *were* old. They still kept doing things old people shouldn't and falling over and being surprised. Grandpa had fallen off the cowshed roof quite recently, where he had been replacing slipped tiles. He was eighty-five.

Drakesend, where they lived, had been farmed by Grandpa and his father before him. It was halfway up what passed for a hill in these lowland parts, between the tidal river below and the wooded brow of the old parkland above. The house looked very picturesque, with its oak timbering infilled with bricks in patterns and its sagging roof of old brown tiles, but it was uncomfortable to live in, having no central heating and lots of cold, stone-flagged passages. Sandy always thought it ought to have ghosts, but no apparitions, friendly or otherwise, had ever disturbed her sleep. She assumed she wasn't sensitive enough to pick up their vibrations. In the bottom corner of the window in her bedroom, engraved on the glass, was a spidery signature: Hannah Rosewall, and the date, 1776. Sandy thought of Hannah Rosewall when she lay in bed during the light summer evenings and wondered what her life was like at Drakesend in 1776. But absolutely no visions came to haunt her.

Below the house were the old brick yards that dated back a century or two, but Bill Fielding, Sandy's father, had built a modern block of barns alongside the old ones, and a new milking parlour for the cows. The best of the old yards he had fitted out as stables and set up as a do-it-yourself livery yard, his gesture towards 'alternative farming'. He more or less left the running of it to Sandy – 'You're the horsy one round here' – but as some of the customers were twice or three times her age and thought they knew everything, they didn't take kindly to being told what they should do by a young girl. The best thing about it was that her schoolfriend, Leo, kept her pony in the yard and came down every evening on her bike.

At least they could do what they liked with their own spare time and their own ponies.

Unlike Julia, whose mother met her off the school bus in her second-best Rover and rushed her home to change into her jods and get some schooling in. Without even having any tea.

Minnie, short for Big Gun from Minnesota, which was the pony's registered name, was tied up in his loosebox, already saddled and bridled. A brown gelding of just under fourteen two hands, he was mostly thoroughbred and extremely good-looking. His winter coat, just coming through, was dense as mole fur and shone with good health and over-feeding; his neat oiled hooves jigged impatiently over the floor, eager to go. As usual, Julia's heart sank at the sight of him, instead of lifting with eager anticipation.

'Take him for a good long hack,' her mother ordered. 'We won't jump him tonight, so he won't get too wound up for tomorrow.' Tomorrow night he had to compete under floodlights in an indoor arena some twenty miles away. They would not get home before eleven, and Julia would fall asleep in the horsebox. Just hacking was, in effect, a rest-cure.

Sandy's remark in the bus had upset Julia.

Everyone at school thought she was stuck-up and a show-off, but it was only how her parents made her seem, not how she herself wanted to be. Her brother Nick and sister Petra were very competitive and sharp but both had left school now and Julia was too young to join in with their activities, nor did she want to. She had few friends, not even Minnie who bit her as soon as looked at her. Sandy's pony, George, although useless, looked for Sandy over the gate with his ears pricked and his upper lip quivering with devotion. Julia had seen him, and envied.

Sometimes she thought she would like it if she had a pony like George. She only wanted to go down through the lanes and the water-meadows to the sea-wall and ride along by the river, watching the geese and the odd yacht. Dreaming. Wishing she didn't have to win. Wishing she wasn't the odd man out in her family. Wishing she had time to go out with other girls, or just mess about with someone else, doing nothing in particular, like Sandy and Leo. But even when she just hacked out she couldn't wander along and dream, because Minnie was forever fighting for his head, snatching at his bit and pulling her arms out of their sockets. When he felt grass underfoot he went, whether she willed it or not. Julia was a good rider but her bravery grew thin sometimes. It was no fun fighting all the way, and being carted.

She went out along the road and down the lane past Flirtie Gertie's cottage towards the river. She was fairly sure she wouldn't meet Sandy, for Drakesend lay on its own lane which forked off left just past Gertie's, and the track she chose went straight down. Minnie walked like a cat on hot bricks, tucking his nose in and switching his tail irritably. The ground was hard after the long hot summer and Julia knew she mustn't gallop if she could help it: it would be bad for the pony's expensive legs. Not on this hard-baked track, at least. She let out her rein cautiously, wanting to relax the pony, but he only snatched the more, poking out his nose and walking faster and faster.

'Oh, I hate you!' she snapped.

She was hungry and tired, and just wanted to enjoy the lovely evening. Self-pity swamped her. She had no friends, no kind, understanding mother, no super brother – like Sandy. Her mother was hard as iron, an ex-showjumper who now used her children to pursue the sport instead of doing it herself. Nick and Petra seemed to enjoy it and Julia had when she was younger, but now she had to ride Minnie she hated it. Minnie was brilliant, and when they didn't win it was always her fault, not Minnie's – her fault for not making the turn tighter, her fault for not taking a steadying pull, her fault for asking for an extra stride. Her mother expected her to win. Her mother was a bad loser. Her mother hadn't bought her Big Gun from Minnesota to come second.

'And you don't like me, you pig, do you?' she said out loud, and gathered up her reins and sent him on at a swinging trot down the grassy path. He had beautiful paces – if only his temperament were as sweet! She wouldn't let him canter because she knew he would buck.

She let him scramble up the sea-wall, and stopped him for a moment to look down the river. The tide was out and the river – called the Branklet – was only a channel between banks of shining mud. The Branklet wound lazily across the marshes, a small tributary of the big river, the Brank, some three miles away which went directly out to sea. The Branklet was navigable at high tide to some three or four miles beyond Drakesend, and one or two fishing boats came in and out when the water was there; small yachts came up to anchor so that their crews could walk up to the pub over the fields. There was a grass-covered wall on either side which was lovely to ride along, and the marsh below was patterned with reeds and ditches frothing with meadow-sweet and ancient hawthorns gnarled from the east wind. Julia liked things like that, unlike her mother. Her mother thought there was nothing to beat riding in a menage with rails round it. She only sent Julia on hacks to try and 'let down' the evil Minnie. Tomorrow it would be the floodlit show-jumping arena again.

In the summer if the water was high on a hot day, Sandy and Leo would ride their ponies down to the wall and turn them loose while they had a swim. Julia had seen them. Imagine doing that with Minnie!

Minnie was tired of her dreaming and started to pull again. The turf on the top of the wall was springy and full of flowers. Julia's arms ached so she gave up holding on and let Minnie go. As she galloped, she thought how much she hated all this action and spite, and wished with all her heart she could just lie in the grass until the sun went down over the trees behind Drakesend. And never go show-jumping again.

'I say, look at Julia go!'

Sandy and Leo were getting two of the horses in from the bottom field. (Do-it-yourself was a somewhat lax term, several of the owners much preferring Sandy to 'do it', rather than 'themselves'.) As they walked down, swinging the headcollars, they could see the distant Big Gun from Minnesota tearing along the sea-wall in the distance.

'The clock goes back at the end of the month,' said Sandy. 'She won't come down here then.'

Sandy didn't like meeting Julia when she rode out. Julia always gave her a terrible inferiority complex. Minnie was so brilliant, and dear George would amble along while Minnie went on springs. Sandy didn't know what it felt like to ride a pony like Minnie, and was aware of her ignorance. She supposed she knew as much about looking after and handling horses as Julia, because Julia's place had grooms. But there was nothing impressive about that, compared with show-jumping.

'I wouldn't like to be Julia, all the same,' Leo said, guessing her thoughts. 'You don't enjoy things you've *got* to do. We only do this because we like it. We haven't got to.'

'Speak for yourself ! Miss Ball asked me to get them in. She can't come down tonight!'

'She's a bit batty, Miss Ball. The weather's beautiful. Why bring them in?'

'Because the little darlings like their beddy-byes. You know her.'

Miss Ball was a retired school teacher who had bought a black mare, which she christened Blackie ('Oh, the imagination!' cried Sandy's mother), at a car-boot sale. She brought it to Drakesend and hacked happily around until, one morning, Blackie was found with a foal beside her. This was called Surprise. Miss Ball was over the moon with delight, in spite of having to pay two liveries, and now doted on her couple like a mother hen. Miss Ball, who was short and round, had a friend called Miss Stitchman, who was tall and thin. Sandy's father called them Stick and Ball.

The girls put Blackie and Surprise in their adjoining boxes where large haynets were hanging ready for them. Most of the horses were still at grass, the weather was so mild. Their clients were nearly all pottering sorts of riders. There were only one or two who rode seriously: a rather spectacular young woman with red hair called Polly Marlin, who had an eventer, and a spotty-faced but talented boy called Henry, her pupil, who wanted to be world champion at dressage. He was saving up to buy his dream horse, which he reckoned would cost about ten thousand pounds. In the meantime he was making do with a one-eyed mare from the Rescue who was already doing flying changes and a crabwise progression known as *passage*, which was quite impressive.

Sandy and Leo went into the tackroom to hang up the headcollars, and then up the ladder into their private domain, the old hayloft above the tack and feedroom. They had their own kettle up here and had furnished it with thrown-out chairs and an old feed-bin for a table. Everyone knew better than to join them, and the customers would stand at the bottom and shout if they wanted Sandy. They had their own kettle and coffee things below.

Leo (short for Leonie) wasn't allowed to have animals at home, her parents being very clean and particular, so she spent most of her time at the farm, mucking out and messing about. Luckily she was very clever and could do her home-work in a trice, so her parents couldn't complain. She was a thin, earnest-looking girl with large spectacles and sparky brown eyes. Her hair was straight and fell down on either side of her face so that she was forever pushing it back, looking as if she was peering out of a thicket. She was brilliant at maths and science and hadn't a hope of not going to university and becoming a professor in the years ahead, but she loved Drakesend and wanted to be a farmer. Sandy didn't know what she wanted to be. Happy, really.

Sandy put the kettle on and Leo crossed over to the opening that looked out over the yard and down to the river. She leaned her head against the jamb.

'Do you think he'll come tonight?'

'No. Not up here. Along the sea-wall, perhaps.'

'Who is he?'

'Nobody else has noticed him, only us.'

'Julia has. She's seen him. Not close though. If he sees you, she says, he gallops off.'

'He rides at night, in the moonlight!'

'I wish I'd seen him!' Leo said.

'On the sea-wall, in the moonlight, on that grey horse! It looked fantastic!'

Sandy's bedroom faced the river and she had looked out, without putting the light on, and seen a rider on a grey horse galloping over the marshes, silhouetted against the wide, silver spread of the river at high water. Once the rider had come up the lane from the river and galloped past Flirtie Gertie's in the dusk, but even then she never got a good look at him. It was a boy, they could see that, thin and dark, on a grey thoroughbred. He rode without a saddle and with only a rope halter as far as she could see.

'The wild boy!' Leo sighed. 'Who is he?'

'Dad says he must be a gypsy.'

'There aren't any gypsies around here, not that I know of.'

'And where does he keep the horse?'

'Perhaps he'll bring it here!'

It was their dream to have a Magic Male, with a magnificent horse, to upgrade their yard. The only males so far were Henry and a bumbling old man they called Uncle Arthur with his ewe-necked chestnut mare, Empress of China. ('Now that's a splendid name!' said Sandy's mother. 'That's noble!' 'But you should just *see* her!' the girls wailed. *'Empress!'*)

'We've absolutely got to meet him,' Leo said firmly.

'Catch him!'

Sandy laughed. 'George isn't fast enough!'

'Julia could, on Minnie.'

'How sickening, if she gets to know him!'

They made coffee, dreaming their dreams. Their mothers thought ponies kept their minds off boys.

Before they had finished, they heard the sound of a lorry coming up the lane behind the yard. There were useful cracks in the timbering of the old loft which gave them a lookout across the lane, so they investigated.

'Horsebox! No-one we know.'

'It's got a horse in, hark at it kicking!'

'New customer.'

'We're not expecting anyone.'

'It's a man!'

'Stopping.'

'Getting out . . .'

'Let's go down!'

They scrambled down the ladder into the yard and out through an archway which gave on to the lane and the house. The horsebox driver turned round and greeted them.

'I say, can I leave a horse here?'

He was young, about eighteen, and had a very educated voice, and a superior, bossy manner. He was rather handsome in a stuck-up way, with very blue eyes and close-curling but severely cut hair. Both girls stared at him, trying to work out if he could possibly be the Magic Man. There was a lot in his favour, but his approach was damning.

'Who runs this place?'

Sandy straightened up to her full, impressive five foot three and said, 'I do.'

'Have you got a spare box then?'

There was a drill for new customers. If Sandy didn't like the look of them, she said the place was full. If she did, she had to take them up to the house to be vetted and approved.

This time she hesitated.

Leo glanced at her, appalled. 'There's the corner box,' she said.

Sandy gave her a betrayed look.

'I don't know—'

'If it's empty tonight, I'll take it,' the man said peremptorily. 'I'll probably find something better when I've had a chance to look round. I got this horse rather unexpectedly – my great-aunt died and left it me, and her head groom sent it down without any advance warning. Stupid thing to do. It's been travelling all day.'

It was the nearest he could get to an appeal.

'Oh, poor thing,' said Leo. 'Can we look at it?'

Before the man could say anything, she had opened the groom's door and climbed up. Sandy followed her. They looked up and saw a head, very high up, looking over a partition, arrogant of expression and noble in profile. Definitely out of the George and Blackie league. Not the sort of horse they were used to at all. Seeing the faces in the doorway, the horse whinnied imperiously. It was a dark chestnut with a white stripe on its face, and must have been at least seventeen hands high. Its eyes were large and bold and agitated. The horsebox rocked as it stamped its feet.

They were very impressed.

Leo hissed, 'You must take it!'

'The man's horrible!' Sandy hissed back.

'But look at the horse!'

Sandy knew that opportunities should be seized. How did she know that this young man hadn't got a heart of gold underneath the arrogant manner? Very shy people sometimes gave a bad first impression, she remembered her mother telling her. You think they're stuck-up, but really they're shy.

'My name's Anthony Speerwell. I live at Brankhead.'

Leo gave Sandy a violent nudge. The Speerwells of Brankhead were well known, having made a lot of money out of development and speculation in nearby towns. Unlike most builders, Mr Speerwell had thrived even through hard times. He had bought the lovely old Brankhead House in order to turn it into flats, but it was listed and he couldn't get planning permission. Sandy's father said he must have thought he could 'buy' permission, but so far he hadn't managed it, so had moved in with his family. Instead of being bowled over with joy, Mrs Speerwell kept complaining about being too far away from Marks and Spencer.

Leo's nudge nearly knocked Sandy over.

'Tonight,' Sandy said. 'There's a spare box. But I can't promise—'

'I'll unbox him then.' (No grateful thanks, no charming smile.)

'We've got to get the stable ready first.'

'I'll wait then.' (No offer to help.)

'What's the horse called?' Leo asked.

'King of the Fireworks. He's said to be one of the best hunters in Leicestershire.'

'Cor!' said Leo.

'You are a *creep*!' Sandy railed as they went to fetch the straw. 'The Speerwells are horrible! Everyone knows that!'

'He's terribly handsome. And the horse looks fabulous. I thought we wanted some class around here? Blackie – and Empress of China – I ask you! Henry's one-eyed Dodo—' Her voice was deeply scornful. 'How are you going to attract class horses if you turn away the only decent—'

'Oh, shut up! The horse is all right – but *him*! Anthony Speerwell – Sneerwell, more like it!'

It was going dark. Sandy switched the yard lights on and they humped four bales of straw from the barn into the empty corner box between Blackie and Empress of China. Empress of China stuck her ewe neck over the door and watched with interest. They filled a large haynet and put it up, and Sandy staggered across the yard with two water buckets, then they went back to the lorry, where Anthony Sneerwell was sitting in the cab, smoking.

'It's ready.'

'You've been a long time.'

'This is a do-it-yourself yard,' Sandy said crossly. 'Didn't you know? It's not our job.'

'I can pay you.'

He stubbed out his cigarette and got down. The girls stood back as he let down the rear ramp of the lorry. Sandy wanted to see if he knew anything about horses, as she rather suspected he didn't. King of the Fireworks was crashing around inside, obviously thinking it was time he was released, and she saw Anthony hesitate as he went to reach up to undo the headcollar rope. She saw that the horse, untied, was going to leap out headlong, and ran up the ramp just in time to hang on.

'Steady on!'

The horse all but lifted her off her feet, but she stopped him from plunging out in a heap, and made him look what he was doing. Anthony just held the end of the rope. The horse picked his way down the steep ramp and stood looking about him, head up. Leo's eyes were gleaming with excitement. In the dusk, even under his rugs, the horse had an undoubted quality: both blood and substance, with a beautiful head and bold, enquiring eyes. He looked all round and whinnied.

'Shall I take him?' Sandy asked – but knew at once it was a mistake. Anthony was not going to submit to a girl.

He didn't reply but marched ahead, and Sandy

could see straightaway that he was not experienced with horses, although the horse was
too well-mannered to play him up. It was nervous though, in a new yard, and it was only
when Sandy took the head-rope that the horse
consented to enter the prepared box.

Perhaps Anthony realized that he had been
found wanting, for he showed no sign of wanting
to stop and gloat over his new acquisition, but
turned to go.

'You have to look after him,' Sandy said
anxiously. 'You'll come up in the morning to
feed him and exercise him?'

'I'll probably find a better place tomorrow.
Yes, I'll be back.'

He departed without a word of thanks.

'I don't believe it! That anyone can be so rude!'
Sandy raged. The responsibility was hers if he
didn't come. She was quite sure he knew nothing
about mucking out. 'A better place! Not for what
we charge! The cheek of it!'

She was deeply insulted by the boy's arrogance.
But the horse was gorgeous.

'You have to admit, he's a winner,' Leo sighed.
'Don't send him away!'

Leo thirsted to have lovely things in her life.
Her pony was a scrawny little roan gelding called
Puffin which she adored, because he was a goer
and honest and wanted to please, but he was no
looker. Her parents could not afford the likes of

26

Big Gun from Minnesota, could hardly afford the modest livery charged at Drakesend, but they approved of Leo's interest and had scraped to buy her Puffin. She knew when she was well off, but she couldn't help her dreams.

They gave the new horse a feed from their own store, and then escaped before their liveries came back, pleased to think how amazed they would be when they saw the handsome new head looking over the corner door. King of the Fireworks and Empress of China seemed to have taken to each other and, just managing to touch noses, were whickering lovingly at each other.

'All these names!' Leo said. 'King of this and Empress of that. Let's call ours King George and Prince Puffin.'

'Baron Blackie and Sir Surprise!'

'D – d – Doctor Dodo—'

'*Duke* Dodo.'

They could feel the giggles rising. Leo fetched her bike.

'Goodnight, Lady Leo.' Sandy bowed deeply.

'Goodbye, Senorita Sandy.'

Sandy went indoors. The Fieldings lived mainly in their kitchen, which was large and warm, with a lobby full of muddy gumboots, old jackets and dog baskets. Her father, Bill, wasn't in yet; Ian had been and gone. Mary Fielding was looking in the oven.

Sandy told her about Anthony Speerwell.

'He's absolutely horrid. But it's only for one night.'

'They're not into horses that I know of. Fast cars and big dinner parties is what I've heard.'

'It's a gorgeous horse. He kept saying it's only till he finds something better.'

'There's nowhere better,' Mary Fielding said staunchly. 'More expensive, perhaps.'

'There's nowhere else at all, unless he goes miles.'

It was a remote area. There was no hunting, and the scattered population was not heavily into horses. There was a Pony Club but rather far away, a dealer's yard, and one riding school with quiet hacks.

'It's a pity he's horrid,' Sandy said, and went into a dream about Anthony Speerwell being as gorgeous as his horse, and after a few years falling passionately in love with her and taking her to live at beautiful Brankhead Hall, while his mother removed herself to a Marks and Spencer part of the world.

Sandy went into dreams quite a lot. Much as she adored George, a fat skewbald of thirteen and a half hands (the sort, as Leo pointed out, that was more often to be found on a tether at the side of a road), she hankered after a pony that would win at shows and move like a dancer and turn on its hocks at a touch of the heel. A pony that would cause people to stare and envy, and who would put its trust in her completely, do anything for her, greet her with a loving whinny. George greeted her with a whinny but only if she had a food bucket with her.

Both she and Leo were getting big for George and Puffin now. Neither of their fathers sounded as if they were going to shell out for new ponies, quite understandably, as they seemed to find it hard to pay for boring necessities like blazers and shoes and a hockey stick, not to mention a new car. Sandy knew better than to mention it. She knew she was lucky. But the Julia Marsdens of this world . . . ! Sandy knew that her remark in the school bus had been provoked by jealousy, and felt ashamed. Julia had everything and hated it. What was there to be jealous of?

Disturbed, Sandy went upstairs to her room. Sometimes it was hard to know what she wanted – this great, strange, throat-lumpy feeling of longing and longing for she knew not what would take her up and make her head spin: as if she was drifting through outer space amongst the galaxies that were so far away they were a mere blur of paleness in the sky, not even proper stars. Sometimes she wondered why she was Sandy – who had arranged it? – that she should have been born at Drakesend, instead of in Bombay or Japan or Tierra del Fuego. Why did Ian, too, want what he couldn't have, while Duncan, the boy who did the cows, said he would give his right arm to be Ian and have his own farm to inherit? Who arranged all that so badly? God? And why did they have wishes at all, when they were loved and fed and happy, and millions were starving and dying and didn't have so much as a string vest let alone a pony? Why was Anthony Speerwell so horrid when he had everything a rich boy could desire? Why was her sister Josie so happy when she lived in a house without electricity and a lavatory down the garden and had a baby she hadn't meant to? (Actually, there was an answer to that one: she was in love and lived with her lover, Glynn, who laughed a lot and loved her back.)

Nobody knew Sandy had funny thoughts like this: she was known as 'stolid' (not an uplifting word) and unimaginative. She got jobs at school like clearing up sick because she wasn't squeamish and she didn't complain. She was said to be dependable. They liked her. She was boring, she thought. They didn't like Julia, but Julia was spirited and pretty and temperamental, not *stolid*. They liked Leo but found her confusing because she was quirky and too clever and sometimes malicious in her teasing way; they were never sure of her, like they were with boring Sandy.

So Sandy, not pleased with herself, gazed out of her bedroom window in the darkness and saw the beautiful scene she was so used to that she really never took it in: the marsh fields seamed with ditches lying like silver threads, and the river

30

winding like a silver serpent in the moonlight.

And on the sea-wall, lit by the moon and the stars, a boy on a pale grey horse galloping, silhouetted against the glittering river.

Sandy sucked in her breath, staring – the Wild Boy! The rider no-one had seen close to, no-one had spoken to, no-one knew about . . . the boy who rode at night. As she watched, he turned the horse and came down the wall in one bound and headed for the lane where Julia had ridden earlier, the lane that came up close to the farm and past Flirtie Gertie's. If she were to go down now, run, she might see him at the corner of the lane, coming up from the river.

Sandy ran. She jumped down the stairs three at a time and ran down the passage and through the kitchen, where her father was just coming in.

'Whatever—?'

But Sandy shoved past and out of the door. She ran as if she were being chased, as fast as she could, past the back of the stables and down the farm drive towards its junction with the lane. She heard the hooves coming up the lane, still galloping, and ran till her heart nearly burst, but all she saw was the tail of the grey horse passing and the silver glint of its flying shoes. There was a slim boy bareback, leaning forward, with black hair flying, and no saddle, and only a rope for a rein: that much Sandy saw, but no more. The horse was gone and the thudding of its hooves receded into the silent autumn night.

There was a mist curling up slowly over the water-meadows and nothing moved again, only a heron kraaked from the reeds, and Sandy walked slowly home.

'Hurry up, Julia! You're number ninety-four, and eighty-five is just going in now – you've got to warm him up!'

It was always a rush, getting home from school, boxing up and getting frustrated in the rush-hour traffic on the way to the Equestrian Centre . . . trying not to forget anything. Once she had forgotten her jodhpurs. Julia scowled as she pulled up Minnie's girths.

'He doesn't need warming up. He needs cooling down!'

'Don't be ridiculous!'

Julia's mother was a hyperactive, leathery lady in her forties who drove her family with passion to achieve the heights in the sport she had once excelled in herself. A bad accident had stopped her riding several years ago but hadn't stopped her drive. She held the dancing Minnie's head while Julia mounted.

'It's your attitude that's wrong, Julia,' her mother snapped.

Julia was perfectly well aware of this. As she rode out of the horsebox area through the big doors into the collecting-ring, she was also perfectly well aware of the spectators' eyes fastening on her entry: Julia Marsden on Big Gun from Minnesota, the one they all had to beat. The big tan-bark indoor ring was occupied by the next ten or so ponies to go, warming up, taking turns over the practice jump. Julia knew them all well, and knew she had only one to fear – a boy called Peter Farmer on a strongly bitted grey gelding called Spaceman. His father had put the practice bar up to a ridiculous height and Spaceman was flicking over it contemptuously.

Julia despised such ritual as showing-off. Father Farmer was an unpleasant goader, interested only in winning (rather like her own mother). Peter was all right, but a bit thick. Julia was not friendly with many of her fellow competitors and knew they thought she was stuck-up too, like the people at school. She rode round miserably, putting Minnie through his beautiful paces, circling in both directions, slowing and quickening, and the spectators leaned over the wall and admired her cool, her professionalism.

It was a cold evening. The ponies' breath smoked in the hangar-like indoor school and the lights glared harshly. From the adjoining arena where the competition was taking place came the familiar frantic thud of hooves, the

34

occasional hollow booming of a falling pole, and the sporadic applause. The usual group of parents and hangers-on clustered round the entrance between the ring proper and the collecting-ring, criticizing and gossiping.

Just as Julia was riding past this group, a competitor came out. The round had been audibly unsuccessful and Julia looked to see who had wrought such disaster on the ring. It was no-one she knew, a slightly too large boy on a sweating bay pony. Not unusually, the parents went to meet him and give him a dressing-down.

'She's useless! The knackers' is all she's any good for!' he shouted at them angrily.

'We paid enough money for it!' they screeched back.

Julia had heard it all before, but this time was struck by the demeanour of the bay pony. In its eyes she saw all the misery she was feeling herself – in fact, far more. She had never seen such utter dejection and bewilderment in a pony's expression. It stood head down, trembling, its tail clamped down like a starving dog's.

Julia half pulled up and the little mare lifted her head, looked at Julia and gave a pathetic little whinny. Its rider, having dismounted, chucked it in the mouth.

'Pig!' Julia hissed.

Whether the boy heard or not, she didn't know. She rode on, disturbed, thrown by the funny little whinny. Ponies didn't whinny like that except for a missing companion, or a food bucket. Perhaps I am the missing companion, Julia thought, with an extraordinary, emotional feeling of empathy towards the ill-treated mare. We both hate it, matie; we're made for each other, Julia thought. What if she asked her mother to buy it? Sell the brutish Minnie and buy her the bay mare? Julia was so excited by this thought that she forgot all about her practice jump and heard her number called before she had even asked Minnie for a canter.

'Are you fast asleep?' her mother shouted at her angrily.

'Oh, go and drown yourself!' Julia shrieked.

She swung Minnie round and rode into the arena. She did two circles at a canter, trying to pull herself together. The course was difficult, the jumps all at angles with lots of sharp turns and awkward distances. She had walked it with her mother earlier and paced out the strides, and her mother had told her exactly how to ride it, but now it all seemed to have gone out of her head. She had a job to find the first jump.

Minnie was bombing underneath her as usual. The bell went to start and she rode down towards a brush and bar and jumped that easily, then on to some rails and then a funny thing that looked like a wall with a pergola over the top. Minnie jumped it so big that Julia nearly hit her head on the archway. Then he took off at a gallop and, by the time she had got him back, they came to a double spread all wrong. Minnie, being the ace he was, put himself right and jumped it well, but then Julia found herself at the top of the arena with a choice of jumps, one to the left and one to the right, and she had no idea which way to go. She chose the one that Minnie, she could feel, was fancying himself but no sooner had they landed than the bell went for wrong course and she was eliminated.

She had never done anything like this in her life before – well, not since she was little. Minnie, eager to carry on, couldn't understand why she was pulling him up and put in some angry bucks.

'What are you dreaming about, Julia? Is it a boy?' asked a friendly steward, but Julia could see her mother waiting, and couldn't appreciate the joke. She was in a complete spin – all because of a distressed bay mare.

She came back into the collecting-ring, passing a grinning Peter Farmer on his way in, and slipped down as her mother came to meet her. She buried her face under the saddle flap to ungirth as her mother let fly.

'You stupid idiot child! Do you think I go to all this trouble to have you throw away your chance because you're too bone idle to concentrate? You walked the course, didn't you? We discussed that turn at the top – don't you remember? Are you plain stupid, or ill, or what? If you're too gormless to ride a course we might as well sell up and call it a day!'

'Do you mean that?' Julia asked, emerging from under the saddle flap.

'Do I mean what? Don't I always mean what I say?'

'Sell him. Sell Minnie?'

'Are you mad?'

'I hate him.'

'You'd never find a pony as good as this anywhere. Don't talk rubbish!'

'You said it! Sell up, you said.'

Julia, bright red, knew this conversation was being conducted in public with a whole collection of interested eavesdroppers. Child riders were commonly dressed down in full view when things went wrong. Mostly, their parents couldn't even have got over the first jump had they been asked.

'It's you that wants to do this, not me!' Julia said furiously. 'Even when it goes right, you know I hate it!'

'I can't believe what I'm hearing!' Julia's mother cried, and with obvious truth. 'We buy you a pony of the calibre of Big Gun from Minnesota, costing a fortune, and you—'

Words failed her.

Julia burst into tears.

'I hate him, and I hate you too!'

She turned blindly away, shoving through the interested, grinning spectators, and rushed out into the darkness. The cold air hit her like a slap. Lights shone from the living quarters of the horseboxes parked on the grass, and showed happy children and happy parents who all loved it, tacking up their ponies and playing with the dog. Lucky beasts! She knew they all envied her, Julia Marsden on the fantastic Big Gun from Minnesota, and she didn't want any of it. She thought of Sandy and Leo giggling on their pathetic ponies as they rode along the sea-wall.

She thought there was something wrong with her. She was fourteen and a total mess. She couldn't stop crying.

She walked down the rows of horseboxes towards a friendly darkness where the trees took over and the cross-country course lay. At the end of the row, as she passed, she heard a familiar voice.

'If you'd buy me a *decent* pony—'

A boy flounced into the back of a horsebox, leaving a bay mare tied to a ring in the side. She was sweating but he didn't even bother to put a rug over her. Julia thought he would come back, but he didn't. He was looking for his sandwiches. His father was laying into him, but Julia couldn't hear the words. In the darkness she went up to the bay pony and put a hand on the damp neck.

The pony pulled back anxiously, as if she expected to be hit.

'No,' Julia whispered. 'It's all right.'

She stroked the quivering neck.

'It's your fault I went wrong. I was thinking about you.'

The mare had a beautiful head, with a small white star. She was just over fourteen hands high, a bright bay with black points. She pulled back to the end of her halter rope and stared at Julia with her sad, frightened eyes.

'I wouldn't hurt you. You're a darling.'

Julia forgot her own misery. She looked carefully at the horsebox in the dark and managed to read the logo on the front. 'Westharbour Stables. Prop: Edward Porter.' The address was local, but Julia had never heard of them. They must be new to show-jumping.

She stroked the mare some more and gave her a solitary pony-nut she found in her pocket. Then, as she heard the boy coming back down the ramp, she faded away into the darkness. She knew she had to go back. She hated the journeys home when things had gone wrong. She hated them even when things had gone right, always so late and her homework undone and trouble looming at school. Her mother said it didn't matter, but that was no excuse with the teachers.

When she got back to the horsebox she found her mother talking to the local dealer.

'No, he's not for sale, not until Julia's out of her class.' She was rugging up Minnie and threw his leg-guards at Julia.

'Where've you been? Get these on.'

'I know what he cost you. You could make five grand. I've got a customer.'

'Yes, I dare say you have. But I'm not interested.'

Julia was, but didn't say.

'Ah, well. If you change your mind—'

'I know where you live, John. But forget it.'

Julia's mother, give her her due, did not carry on for too long even after their most vehement arguments. They did a lot of shrieking at each other, but gained an even keel quite quickly. No doubt her mother had taken a wrong course in her time.

They set off for home.

'Do you know the Porters – Westharbour Stables? He jumped before me.'

'A bay pony? Useless. No, I don't know them. You should count yourself lucky you don't have to go into the ring on rubbish like that.'

'It might have been the riding.'

'Both rubbish.'

'I liked the pony.'

'There's no accounting for taste.'

'I could make it jump. Couldn't I have it?'

'Are you mad?'

Her mother took her eyes off the road and gave her an unbelieving stare.

'When you've got Big Gun? If you want a second pony I'll buy you one, but not a thing like that – I wouldn't have that in my yard!'

'What's wrong with it?'

'Too small for a start. No action. Not straight in front. Bad mouth. I don't know what gets into you, Julia, I really don't! You have such funny ideas.'

It has a heart and a soul, that pony, Julia thought, and it feels like me and we could love each other. But she didn't say any more.

The following week at the centre Julia won and the little bay mare jumped again, getting everything wrong and several hard wallops in punishment. The dealer made another offer for Big Gun which was turned down with the same scorn.

Two nights later, Julia was told to go for a long, steady hack after school. She had been thinking over her life and had come to a decision – that it was now or never, and she rode away from home and headed for the yard of John Partridge, the dealer, which was some five miles away. She had to get home before dark and there was very little time, so she went cross-country, jumping gates and fences. She was very nervous, and taut with excitement, but Minnie went like a train, loving the tension he could feel in Julia and jumping magnificently.

As they turned down the lane to the dealer's yard, Julia leaned forward and stroked Minnie's neck.

'You're a good fellow really. I'm sorry, Minnie, it's not your fault. It's mine.'

She was being a total idiot, she knew. The feel of Minnie jumping beneath her was magnificent, but she wanted something else. As she rode into the yard, she half pulled up, panicking.

But John Partridge, coming out of a loosebox, saw her. He recognized her at once. His face lit up.

'Your mother accepted my offer?'

'No,' Julia said. 'But I would like to.'

'What'll she say to that then?'

'After tonight, whatever happens, I am never going to ride him again. Never. So she'll have to sell him.'

'By gum! You a mutineer all of a sudden?'

'Yes. I hate show-jumping.'

'Yeah, it's a daft game. But I make a good living out of it. What am I to do then? You put me in a bit of a pickle, like.'

'I want another pony in part-exchange. It'll only be cheap, because it's no good. It's a bay mare that belongs to the Porters of Westharbour Stables. It jumps in the same class as me.'

'I know it.'

'If you can get that, I promise you will have Big Gun. I will absolutely refuse to ride him.'

'I buy this pony of Porter's, and I get this 'un in part-exchange?'

'That's right. But remember, the bay pony

43

must be cheap. My mother won't mind – in the end – as long as she doesn't get done.' Julia knew her mother well.

John Partridge rubbed his chin doubtfully. He was sharp, like most dealers, not dishonest; he had a good reputation. But . . .

'This is a funny do. You're a minor. I can't do a deal with a kid.'

'No. The cheque will be for my mother. It's perfectly straightforward.'

'Aye, well, it's a rum idea. But it would suit me. I'd like it to work, same as you. I've got a real good home waiting for this fellow if you want to sell 'im. German gentleman. Wants the best.'

'You'll do it?'

'Aye, I'll take a gamble. I'll see if I can get the mare – give Porter a ring tonight.'

'If you do, I'll bring Minnie over at once and collect the mare. I won't say anything to my mother.'

'Gawd save us – she's not going to like it!'

'If she's got no rider, Minnie's no good to her.'

'Too right.'

'And I mean what I say. I won't let you down.'

She sat up straight in the saddle and looked challengingly at the dealer. She was only small for her age and had large violet eyes like a filmstar, very white skin and jet-black hair. John Partridge thought she looked a treat: as pretty as the pony and just about as clever. He could not help a big smile.

'You're a rum gel.' He winked amicably. 'We'll see if we can do a deal then. I'll get on to Porter.'

'I'll ring you tomorrow and find out how you got on. Don't ring me!'

'Right you are!'

Julia rode home, her blood racing. She was so excited, and frightened, by what she had done, that she forgot about the time and rode home by the lanes, in a dream. It was dark for the last two miles and passing cars swore at her as they swerved to see the dark pony's tail in their headlights. Julia swore back.

'Pig! Roadhog! Horses came first!'

She was in the wrong, she knew, but her blood was up. She enjoyed screaming in the darkness. She had to make an excuse for being late. Her mother was furious, as she knew she would be.

'I thought he was a bit tender in front, so I walked all the way home.'

'You should have led him!'

'It's not that bad. I'm not sure if it's anything at all.'

'Let's have a look. Which leg?'

'Near.'

Julia raced indoors and up to her room, leaving Minnie with her mother. Her mother liked looking after horses better than people. Something was burning in the oven by the smell of it, but tonight Julia had no appetite. She was away with her dreams, having the little bay mare to love and ride down by the river and not go show-jumping ever again. She lay on her bed shivering, although it wasn't cold, and then got up and looked out of the window. There was a bright harvest moon, low and orange and very unreal-looking, that lit up the back garden and the woods at the bottom. There was a path that led through the woods and came out on the ridge that over-looked the river. The land the other side of the wood was Drakesend's, once an old park, now the grazing that Bill Fielding used for his cows, and you could ride down to the river and all the way out down to the estuary if you turned right, and all the way up to the fishing village of Riverhead if you turned left.

The Marsden house was large and new, up a wide asphalt drive from the road, with the stables at the side. It was very soldierly and smart, with bedding plants in front and nothing up the red-brick walls. It was on the edge of the village. Further along towards the river was the village proper – only a few houses along the road, with a shop and a pub, not much of a village at all. Leo lived next to the village shop, in an ex-farmworker's cottage. It had a big garden, although the house was tiny. Her father was a mad gardener and had flowers sprawling in all directions and the cottage covered with climbers so that there was hardly any architecture to be seen. Julia didn't like Leo: she was too clever by half and made spiky jokes. Sandy was all right. They had been talking in school about a new livery that had arrived called King of the Fireworks. It belonged to Anthony Speerwell.

'Whatever is he thinking of, taking a horse like that to Drakesend Livery?' her mother had said in tones of shock.

'A horse like what?'

'King of the Fireworks – must be the same horse – is, or certainly was, a great team-chaser. From Leicestershire? Must be the same one. Not the sort old Bill Fielding's used to in his cow byres.'

'Sandy said Anthony Speerwell can't ride. He thinks he can. He gets carted all the time, or bucked off.'

'What a tragedy!' (She meant for the horse, not Anthony Speerwell.)

'Her aunt left it to him in her will.'

'What a stupid thing to do! She was a great old biddy, a hunting lady, rode till she was eighty-five. Perhaps her brain went.'

'Perhaps she thought he could ride. He tells everyone how good he is, Sandy says. He says it's the horse that's no good.'

'Well, don't they all?'

'He can't sell it because if he doesn't compete on it he won't get the money she's left him. She's left him a lot,' Sandy said, 'but only if he takes up team-chasing.'

'I don't believe this!'

'That's what Sandy said. Leo says it's obvious the old lady could see how spoilt and revolting he is and on her deathbed tried to think of a way of improving him.'

'Improving him! Team-chasing! He'll break his neck, more like! I find this story hard to believe.'

So did Julia, but that's what she had been told. Team-chasing was a sport where four horses went cross-country together: they were timed, and the fastest team was the winner. It was very hairy and not for fainthearts.

Julia had always rather fancied Anthony Speerwell, having met him once when taken by her parents to a Christmas drinks party at Brankhead Hall. But Sandy and Leo called him Anthony Sneerwell and said he was foul.

She felt very edgy about the plan she had put in motion, and was sick after breakfast the next day. Her mother said she had better stay away from school, but that was the last thing she wanted. She forced herself to get better and tore out for the school bus, sitting alone in the front seat and wondering how soon she dare ring up John Partridge. Sandy and Leo were giggling across the aisle, and Ian Fielding sat alone behind them, staring into space. He quite often came and sat with Julia, but not in the mornings when he hardly spoke to anyone. He was very moody. Julia liked him a lot, but he didn't seem interested in girls.

The morning dragged interminably, but Julia would not let herself ring up before lunchtime. As soon as the end-of-morning bell went, she raced for the call-box in the school lobby.

She had been careful to bring the right coins, and Mr Partridge's number was engraved on her mind.

'Hello! Hello! It's Julia Marsden. Did – did you—?'

'Oh, I thought you might have thought better of it!'

'No! No! Of course not! Did you see Mr Porter?'

'Aye. He's quite agreeable.'

'Oh!' Julia felt as if she were going to take off, suddenly light-headed with relief.

'He's asking two thousand but I'll get him down from that, don't you fret. I'm going over this evening. If it's a deal I can run her straight over if it suits you.'

'No, don't do that!'

She needed breathing space. She felt sick again. Her hand was sticky on the receiver.

'I – I'll ride over on Big Gun, take the mare back.'

'When will that be?'

'Er – when – when – I can. Saturday perhaps.'

'You'll not let me down, I hope!'

'Oh no, I wouldn't do that.'

She rang off. She didn't see how on earth she was going to do it! They were going to a show on Saturday, leaving mid-morning, and the evenings were now too short: her mother wouldn't let her hack out any more. She realized that she didn't know anything at all about the little bay mare. She might be hopeless on the road, or nappy, or be unsound. She didn't even know how old she was – she might be eighteen! Julia kept going hot and cold in turn, and shivering.

On Saturday morning, they were taking Nick's and Petra's horses as well and going to a show near Cambridge. It would make sense to go to the show and ride Minnie over on Sunday morning, but Julia could not bear the thought of doing another show. She decided to go out early on the Saturday, before anyone else was up. If she went out the back way her mother wouldn't see her: her bedroom was in the front, looking down the drive. Petra and Nick wouldn't wake up if the roof fell in, only when their shrill alarm clocks went off.

Her mother thought she was ill. She was sick twice more, and couldn't eat. She was terrified, now, of what she was doing. She must be out of her mind! Her mother would storm over to John Partridge and tear his cheque into little pieces. But Julia knew, if she flatly refused to ride Minnie ever again, her mother would be powerless. Nick and Petra were too old to jump him and the pony was useless without a rider.

On Friday night she couldn't sleep. Then, near dawn, she was terrified of falling asleep and not waking. She got up and went to the window. It was a very fine morning, with the tip of a red sun showing over the shoulder of the hill that hid the river. The brown ploughland was crimson from the glow of the sky and a pheasant was calling at the end of the garden. Julia forgot all her frights: the moment had come and today she was buying the bay mare. Dear bay mare, be everything I want you to be, Julia prayed to the fiery sky. At last, she didn't feel sick or frightened, only immensely happy and excited.

She crept downstairs and went out to Minnie. She left a note in the manger saying, 'Gone for a ride', then threw off his rugs and tacked him up as fast as she could, before any of the others thought it was feedtime and started whinnying. Then she led him out round the back and through the gate on to the bridle path, mounted and trotted away down the track. There was a hole in the hedge which gave on to a ploughed field and if she turned back the way she had come and followed the hedgerow she could go back past her house to the road. Her mother got up early, but not this early. Julia felt pretty sure she would not be seen.

Now that she had done the tricky bit, her heart soared. She rode fast, loving it, even Minnie's arm-wrenching pulling and plunging and jinking and shying.

'Bad luck, poor little German who gets you,' she said to him, sitting an enormous shy as a pheasant went up from under his feet. 'Perhaps he will teach you some manners.'

She had never managed it, not for want of trying. When she got to the dealer's yard and dismounted, Minnie turned round and snapped at her, taking a large bite out of her quilted jacket. Julia was pleased. If he had turned affectionate and pathetic on her, she would have felt bad – but affection and pathos were not in his nature.

'He's a grand jumper, all the same,' said Mr Partridge, laughing. 'I'll warn the German gentleman. But he'll not be bothered. Most fine horses have a bit of spirit.'

He had a box waiting for him, and some spare rugs. Julia took off the saddle and bridle.

'The mare—?'

'I've got her in the end box. She's quite an ordinary pony, you know. I don't know why you would swap this grand fellow for her. I beat Porter down to just over the thousand, so your mother's not getting a bad deal. Tell her I'm not passing your pony on at once, so she can come and talk it over with me if she's upset about it. I don't want to get on the wrong side of your mother, you understand. I've me reputation to think about.'

'It will be all right, I promise!' Julia said wildly. All that was still to come. 'I must see the mare!'

She ran down to the end box and looked in. The mare was standing in the far corner, very nervous and miserable. She looked tucked up and thin. She lifted her head and turned towards Julia, her large eyes expectant and fearful. Julia slid the bolt back. She moved very quietly and spoke softly, holding out her hand. The mare shifted uneasily and put back her ears. Julia reached her and put a hand on her damp neck.

'What have they done to you?' she whispered.

She stroked the mare steadily. The ears came forward and the mare put her muzzle against Julia's chest and rubbed her.

'Ah, you've a way with her. She's very nervous. She's no chicken, you know – twelve, by my judgement. She was a good pony in her day but she got into wrong hands.'

'What's her name?'

'Faithful.'

'Oh, that's a good name!' Not like Big Gun from Minnesota.

'She used to jump. I remember her when she was young. Bin ruined by bad riding, I dare say. Or over-pressed. Lost her confidence.'

Julia put the saddle and bridle on. She would have forgotten all about the money, but Mr

Partridge said, 'I've a cheque to make out to your mother. Just hang on a minute.'

Julia led the mare out into the yard and mounted. She couldn't wait. The mare, although much the same size as Minnie, felt much smaller, being finer and without Minnie's ebullience. She just stood still, head down, not moving. Julia couldn't believe it. She leaned forward and stroked the quivering neck.

'That boy must have been beastly to you,' she whispered.

She knew she must be much lighter than the boy. (Perhaps Minnie wouldn't pull a heavier rider about so. However, it was academic now: she no longer owned him.) Mr Partridge came out with the cheque which she zipped into her pocket; he bade her good luck, and she set off down the drive.

She did not know what she had expected, but she had ridden nothing but Minnie for so long that she had forgotten what a normal pony felt like. No prancing, no pulling, no head-tearing and bouncing, but a placid walk, looking to neither left nor right. No problems. Perfect peace. She could look at the landscape, now basking in the still-reddish light of the early sun, and listen to the birds singing in the hedge and the seagulls wheeling behind a ploughing tractor. The pony's ears were smaller than Minnie's and seemed further away because the neck was relaxed; the mane was thicker, less pulled, and parted untidily on both sides of the neck. For the first half of the ride home Julia felt she was riding on a cloud of happiness. Then, as she started to get close, she had to face the fact that the moment of truth was nearly upon her: her mother was not going to like it. Her mother was going to be very, very angry. All along she had accepted this, but now the deed was done and the music about to be faced, she knew she was really frightened.

She rode very slowly up her home drive and into the yard.

Fair pandemonium reigned, as always when the three of them were boxing up to go to a show. Nick and Petra were shouting at each other and her mother was standing with a face like thunder by the ramp of the horsebox. She heard the hooves approaching and bounded out round the box, looking furious.

'Where've you been? What on earth do you think you're playing at?' She then gaped at the pony in total incredulity. 'Whatever—? What are you doing? Where's Big Gun?'

'I've sold him,' Julia said.

She saw Nick and Petra's faces collapse in shock. She was unable to look at her mother. Wicked delight sparked in her brother's eyes as he exchanged glances with Petra. Julia could see quite clearly that they were both stunned with admiration, which heartened her considerably.

'Here's the cheque. You haven't been done.'

She unzipped her pocket and held out the envelope. Her mother snatched it from her hand.

'John Partridge put you up to this!' she screeched.

'No, no! He didn't! It was my idea. I sold him. You can buy him back if you want, but I shan't ride him. Never!'

'Have you gone mad?'

'No.'

'I don't believe this!'

'I told you! I told you I hated Minnie! You would never listen!'

'You don't know what you're talking about! And what's this animal you're sitting on, for goodness sake?'

'It's Faithful, that belonged to the Porters. She was very cheap.'

'I'm not having that rubbish in my yard.'

'I don't want to jump her. I just want her as my pony.'

'Not here. You'll not keep that pony here.'

'What do you mean?'

'Exactly what I say, my girl. That pony will never earn its keep. It's rubbish. We don't have *pets* here, Julia. We have good working animals. Take it back where you got it from.'

'No!'

'Do as I say.'

'I can't!'

'Of course you can. Take it away. I'm going

to a show with Nick and Petra and if that pony's in this yard when I get back, I'll shoot it. You haven't heard the last of this, Julia.'

Julia was stunned.

'It's not *her* fault! You can't turn her out! Where can she go?'

'Oh, come off it, Julia. You're the planner round here. You can surely think of something!'

Her mother flounced round and started chivvying Nick and Petra.

'Come along, we've wasted enough time! Get those horses into the box. Have you put the tack in? Hurry up!'

In five minutes they had gone. Her mother's parting words, as she drove away, were: 'I mean what I say, Julia. Sort it out before I come back.'

The only thing to sort out was what to do with Faithful. No way was she going to fetch Minnie back. Julia took Faithful into Minnie's old box and untacked her, and then sat in the straw and cried. She was swamped with hurt and self-pity and the aftermath of her sleepless nights. Her mother hated her and now she wasn't even going to be allowed to have Faithful.

The mare came over and sniffed at her curiously, and then stood with her nose touching Julia's shoulder, quite still. Her muzzle was soft as velvet. Julia put her hand up and, instead of biting it like Minnie would have done, Faithful gave her a friendly lick. Julia sobbed.

It was a soft, sunny morning, very still. The yard was quiet, almost sleepy, the stables empty, and the only sound was of a distant tractor ploughing. It was so long since Julia had not been to a show on a Saturday morning that it felt strange and unfamiliar, like somebody else's stable. After a little while she gave up crying and staggered to her feet. She put her arms round Faithful's neck and buried her face in the springy black mane.

'I'm not going to take you back, whatever happens.'

But she was sure her mother would not relent. Her mother was a woman of her word. She would accept that Minnie was not the pony for her daughter, when forced to, but would, no doubt, today, be looking for another more suitable.

'But I don't want another!'

She realized that she was very hungry and thought food would make psr brain work better. So she gave Faithful a large slice of hay and went indoors and made herself some breakfast. She was alone in the house, her father away on a building site, so she had the place to herself. She tried to think of somewhere she could take Faithful, even if just temporarily until she had worked things out and, after bacon and eggs and two cups of tea, she realized the answer was quite obvious: she could take her to Drakesend. This solution was a great burden off her mind and she

58

cheered up immediately. She had enough money in her savings to pay for a couple of weeks at least. That would give her time.

The freedom of not having to go to a show was intoxicating. Two whole days of the weekend to herself, to do what she pleased! She felt as if a great weight had been sprung from her bent back. She put the dishes in the dishwasher and ran out to the stables again, tacked up Faithful and set out for Drakesend.

She went out the back way, the long way round through the parkland instead of just down the road and the lane past Flirtie Gertie's. She wanted the ride, time to think, to take in what she had done. Coming out of the woodland at the top, she put Faithful into her first canter over the old springy turf, and the little mare went eagerly but without pulling, like a dream pony. She had no bad in her that Julia could see, but moved easily with a very smooth and comfortable stride. It was so blissful Julia laughed out loud. When she wanted to stop, she just sat down and felt the reins and the pony came back to her – no effort. Julia found this quite mind-blowing after Minnie and could not stop a great idiotic grin bursting out on her face. They went down the hill towards the river under the big oak trees, whose leaves were bright gold against the clear sky. She had the world to herself, no roofs to be seen, only the tower of the old Elizabethan gatehouse at the bottom of the park, where once a drive had entered and curved through the park to Drakesend. It showed now as just a slightly raised grassy track.

The gatehouse tower had been empty for years, but when Sandy's sister Josie had run off with her lover Glynn and had a baby, they set up home there. Mr and Mrs Fielding were only just beginning to talk to Josie again, the baby winning them over. It had been a jolly village scandal at the time. When Julia rode past now, she saw Josie pinning baby washing on the line. Julia thought the story of Josie and her lover living in the Elizabethan tower with their love-child was the most romantic she had ever come across, although she knew none of their parents thought so. The tower was very beautiful, with little mullioned windows looking down the river towards the sea. Round it was an old garden that Josie had brought back to life, so that it was a mass of old roses and flowers in a froth round the base of the tower, with a lawn of turf where once the Elizabethan ladies had walked. In the summer it was so pretty it hurt. Having no water and no electricity was obviously the other side of the coin, but Julia did not think about that. She just felt, as she rode past, that life was so lovely at this minute that she might burst out of her skin. Having Faithful, and thinking of Josie's love-story, and not being at a horse show but riding across this lovely landscape by herself in the sunshine – it was almost too much to take in.

She came down to the river and rode up the bank on to the sea-wall. Hardly anybody came here, save a few people off yachts wanting to stretch their legs, and the cattle grazed the wall so that the top was lovely smooth grass. The tide was fairly high and one or two yachts were coming up, hardly moving in the soft zephyrs, very leisurely. Faithful pricked her ears enquiringly at the white sails, but walked on calmly.

Now she was getting near to Drakesend, Julia's bursting elation started to be tempered by doubts as to the reception she might get. She knew Sandy and Leo didn't like her much. What if Sandy said she couldn't take Faithful? She had ridden off without thinking about that possibility. What if they were out? But usually they came this way to ride, and the day was still so early they probably weren't ready to set off yet. Even so, Julia began to have doubts, dreading the idea of another rejection. Her mother's words had shaken her.

As she came down the sea-wall to join the lane that led up to the village, she was surprised to hear the thud of hooves behind her. She thought it was Sandy and Leo, but it was the boy on the grey thoroughbred. She had never seen him in broad daylight before, nor so close. He pulled up on the wall above her, and she could see that he didn't want to ride past her. He seemed to contemplate turning back, half turning the horse, but then thought better of it and came down the wall in one bound. He went past Faithful at a canter, without a word, not even looking at Julia, and rode ahead of her up the track so fast that he was out of sight behind the high hedges of the upper lane before Julia had properly taken it in.

Who was he?

She thought she knew the face, but couldn't put a name to it. The horse was a rose-grey mare of about fifteen hands, thoroughbred but small, with a flowing mane and tail and wonderful, athletic movement. Although she appeared to be ridden nearly always at a gallop, there was not a speck of sweat on her. She was hard and fit. Julia, typically, had noticed more of the horse than the boy.

When she got to the Drakesend turning she found Sandy and Leo standing there, looking up the lane. They turned to Julia and with one voice said, 'Did you see him?'

'Yes, he passed me.'

'Do you know who he is?'

'No.'

'Did you see him close to? You must have done.'

'Yes.'

'What's he like?'

'Er—' Julia tried to find words for her muddled impression. 'Sort of – well, like a – a rough sort of boy. Looked like a gypsy, save there aren't any round here any more. He was bareback. Fantastic rider.'

'And no bridle?'

'No. Just a rope halter. I don't know how on earth he has any control.'

'But he does, doesn't he? He's amazing.'

'Yes.' Julia pictured the way he had hesitated on top of the wall and swung the mare with his legs, holding her, then asking her for the bound down the bank. He would be ace in the jumping ring.

'He can certainly ride.'

'How old is he, would you say?'

'Oh, bit older than us. Sixteenish.'

'Long hair?'

'No. Well, perhaps it was tied back. Yes, it might have been long. He looked dark – cross, sort of. Wore jeans and a dirty jersey. He didn't look at me, or say anything.'

'We thought he had long hair.'

The two girls looked dreamy and Julia saw that they had a 'thing' about the boy and were hoping he was everything they were looking for in life. Julia doubted if he would fit the bill. They looked at each other and giggled a bit, then Sandy said, 'Who's that you're riding?'

'It's my new pony. I bought it myself. I part-exchanged Minnie. And my mother won't have it in her yard, she said, so I rode over to ask if I can keep her here.'

Both girls were obviously impressed.

'What, you part-exchanged Minnie without telling your mother?'

'Yes.'

'Cor.' Everyone knew Mrs Marsden and her quick temper. 'I *say*! I bet she wasn't pleased!'

'She was furious. Well, I knew she would be.'

Sandy had a nasty feeling that her remark on the bus might have sparked off this awesome act of rebellion. She felt her blushes mounting at the thought. The new pony was nice, standing quietly while they talked, not jigging about on springs as Minnie would have been.

'Could I keep her here, as a paying livery?'

'Well, yes. We've got room.'

Even as she said it, Sandy could see that her close friendship with Leo could be threatened. Three was always awkward, two pairing against one, and could she be sure it would always be herself and Leo, the pair? Or would Julia keep herself to herself, as she did at school? And if the Magic Man ever turned up, Julia would be the attraction, she was so pretty. Sandy blushed some more, thinking such unworthy thoughts. Julia was welcome to Anthony Sneerwell.

Just as she thought this, Anthony's car appeared at the top of the lane. He came down, driving too fast, and pulled up beside them. He stuck his head out of the window.

'Who's that cretin on the grey? One of your mob?'

'No.'

'I nearly hit him. Riding like a maniac – had the cheek to make a rude gesture at me.'

Leo said, 'Good,' under her breath, and Sandy said, 'Have you come to ride? I haven't put your horse out.'

'Yes, I have.'

'Try to,' Leo said as he put his car noisily into gear and drove on into the yard.

'Come and watch,' Sandy said in a friendly tone to Julia. 'It's great fun.'

'A laugh a minute,' Leo said.

Heartened by the friendly invitation, Julia followed them into the yard.

Sandy showed Julia a spare loosebox and let her get on with putting down the bedding. She went back to Leo and said, 'Cor, what've we let ourselves in for?'

'I thought you said we were full, after King of the Fireworks?'

'That end box is big enough for a pony. And Uncle Arthur keeps saying he's going to give up. He hardly ever comes these days.'

'If he takes Empress of China away, poor old Fireworks'll pine. He's in love with her.'

'I know. That's half Mr Sneerwell's trouble.'

'Are we going to help him?'

'Someone will have to!'

Anthony Speerwell had not yet had a satisfactory ride on King of the Fireworks. The big hunter, having fallen in love with the mare in the adjoining box, was unhappy about leaving her and, when saddled and bridled, refused to leave the yard. Any good rider would soon sort him out but the horse knew, as soon as Anthony got on him, that he had **no** authority. Twice, Sandy and Leo had led him away down the lane until he was out of earshot of the Empress's shrill love-calls. Anthony did not seem to be ashamed of having to be led by little girls: he called the horse a 'thicko' and a 'nutter' and never seemed to think any of it might be his fault.

'He's got a skin as thick as a rhinoceros,' Leo said. 'He'd never believe you if you told him he can't ride.'

'When he's fallen off enough times it might sink in.'

They sat in the tackroom and discussed Julia's revelations, and decided that mummy Marsden would soon relent and have the pony home.

'I don't think she'll trouble us for long,' Leo said.

'She can't be all that bad, doing that, swapping Minnie,' Sandy said. 'Very brave.'

'Hmm,' said Leo.

They waited until the clatter of hooves going backwards and angry shouts told them Anthony was aboard and trying to leave the yard. They looked out. Julia had come out of her pony's box and was watching critically.

'He's got a screw loose, this horse,' Anthony said disparagingly.

'Make him walk on,' Julia said.

'I'm trying, aren't I?'

Julia shrugged.

Anthony gave Fireworks a wallop with the hunting crop he always brought with him, and Fireworks gave an almighty buck so that Anthony landed up the horse's neck. Fireworks then ducked his head and Anthony slid gently down on to the ground. Fireworks turned round and went to slobber over Empress of China, looking lovingly over her door.

Julia said something scathing to Anthony which Sandy and Leo didn't hear. They heard Anthony say, 'If you know everything, you ride him then.'

'All right,' said Julia.

She went to Fireworks, led him away from the Empress and, although he was so tall and she so small, mounted him with apparently no trouble at all. She then walked him calmly and without any fuss out of the yard and into the lane.

'You want him now?' she called back.

Sandy and Leo exchanged glances. It was very impressive.

Anthony shouted, 'Well, he's given in, hasn't he? He only does it for a minute or two.'

He lumbered away in pursuit, dressed in his best hacking clothes. He always came looking as if he was going to a show. Sandy and Leo couldn't understand why he wasn't mortified with embarrassment at being shown up by Julia, but obviously his rhinoceros skin was undented.

Julia came back on her feet, smiling, and went back into Faithful's box, and in a moment King of the Fireworks followed at a smart trot. He went straight over to Empress of China and stuck his head in over her door. Anthony, shooting forward at the sudden stop, hit his head hard on the door lintel. His hat came down over his eyes, badly dented.

Smothering giggles, Sandy and Julia went out to help. Anthony was swearing at his horse, very angry.

'Honestly, all horses do this sort of thing if they get the chance,' Sandy said. 'You've got to be very firm with him. Once he gets the message, he won't try it on any more.'

'He's a lunatic! He's dangerous! How am I going to get a ride if he won't even leave the yard?'

'You'll have to take the Empress with you!'

'She needs exercising,' Sandy said. 'Uncle Arthur hardly ever rides her now, and he doesn't like her being out in the field unless the sun's shining – she's bored rigid.'

'You could ride and lead,' Leo suggested.

'I'll ride her, if you like.' Julia emerged from Faithful's box and made the offer. 'If her owner wouldn't mind, that is.'

'No. He's always asking us to exercise her. Go ahead. I'll fetch her saddle and bridle.'

Neither Sandy nor Leo were keen to ride out with Anthony. They thought Julia's offer pushy but useful. Between them they tacked up the chestnut mare while King of the Fireworks stood waiting hopefully. Empress of China was a clapped-out racehorse of about sixteen and a half hands, fourteen years old, a bright chestnut with a ewe neck and a spine that stuck up however much she ate. She had long rubbery ears and her lower lip hung down, giving her a goofy expression. Her eyes were shrewd; she was intelligent for a horse and not over-eager to please, although she responded to a good rider, which she rarely got.

'She can go bonkers occasionally,' Sandy warned Julia. 'But nothing evil.'

Julia hopped up and the Empress's expression changed to one of surprise. She pulled herself together even before Julia had asked anything, and set off out of the yard with King of the Fireworks at her side.

Sandy and Leo watched them go, not quite knowing what to think.

'Perhaps Julia fancies Sneerwell.'

'She's welcome.'

'He's so handsome! But such a pig! Julia'll find out.'

They were hungry and went into the house for elevenses. The kitchen was full. Josie and Glynn and the baby had just arrived in their Land Rover; Ian was – had been – doing his homework on the kitchen table; Mr Fielding had come in to see Glynn, and Mrs Fielding was dispensing coffee.

Leo, the only child of bookish parents, loved

this big, noisy family kichen with all its coming
and goings. Her house was silent, with only
Radio Three playing quietly in the kitchen. Her
parents only spoke when necessary. The Fieldings
gabbled away all the time. Bill Fielding, having
cut Josie off without a penny and sworn never
to speak to Glynn in his life, was now, a year
later, discussing with Glynn the replacing of a
metal gate on the bottom meadow. Glynn was,
officially, a sculptor (he had met Josie at art
school), but he turned his hand to welding and
carpentry to make a living, and was quite useful
about the farm.

'I've got some old gas-pipe – if the old one
won't mend, I can easily knock up a new one.'

He lolled comfortably at the table, a large blond
man from Liverpool with a conspicuously easy-
going attitude to life. He didn't appear to work
very hard, not like Josie who was always on the
go, decorating, doing the washing, gardening,
looking after the baby and in her spare time
making pottery, which was what she had trained
in. Josie was dark and tense, like Ian. Leo was
very susceptible to Ian, although he was usually
scowling and bad-tempered. She sat down next
to him, but he pulled his books away and made
a great show of being disturbed in the middle of
his work.

'You can go and work in your father's study,'
his mother said to him quietly, but of course he

didn't want to work that badly. Only pretend he did.

'I don't know anybody who does their homework on a Saturday morning,' Leo said conversationally. She did hers on Sunday night. It took her no time at all.

'You haven't got exams,' Ian said darkly. 'Not for years.'

'No, of course, I'm only *little*,' Leo said scathingly.

'Coffee, Leo?' asked Mrs Fielding. She was always calm and unruffled, whatever happened around her; always willing to listen, slow to take sides. Sandy was like her mother. Not ambitious, but utterly reliable. Nice, Leo thought. She didn't think she was as nice. Nor Julia. Sandy had an inferiority complex about being boring. Nobody wanted to be what they were. 'Being nice doesn't mean you're boring,' Leo said, to comfort. Ian was neither nice nor boring.

'Who were those people riding out?' Josie asked. 'New people?'

'Yes. We've got another, Dad,' she added. 'Julia Marsden. She brought a pony this morning. Her mother won't have it.'

'What's wrong with it?'

'Nothing. They've had a row.'

'How many are there now?' Josie asked. 'You must be about full.'

'Eight counting Leo. Nine with me.'

'That's a fair amount of dosh!' Glynn said respectfully.

'It'll be a living for Sandy when she leaves school,' her father said. 'Livery's the thing these days. And she can teach – get a few ponies. Better than farming – it'll pay better.'

'She'll have to get qualified to teach,' Leo said. 'She'll have to go to college.'

'You don't need to go to college to teach kids to ride!'

'You do.'

'Of course you do, Dad,' Josie put in scathingly, to support Leo. 'You've got to be qualified to teach, whatever it is. And certainly to teach riding.'

'Gawd, all these rules! You've got to pass exams to show a kid how to sit with its legs either side of a pony? It's nature, I'd have thought.'

'You sound just like Grandpa!' Josie said, laughing. 'Where is Grandpa, by the way?'

'He's gone up to the village to get some tobacco.'

'Thought it was peaceful.'

'Is that one of yours – lad on a grey pony, always going flat gallop?' Glynn asked Sandy. 'He went past this morning.'

'No. We don't know who he is.'

'He rides like he's stuck on with glue. No saddle either. Where's he come from?'

'Up Riverhead way, we think.'

73

'I know who he is,' Ian said.

'Who then?' Leo pounced.

'Why are you so interested?' He grinned.

Leo bit her tongue. 'Just wondered,' she tossed off. 'It doesn't matter.' Then, because she couldn't help it, she added, 'What's his name?'

'I'm not telling.'

'You don't know!'

'I do. I know his name and where he lives and what he does.'

'Tell us then.'

'No.'

'You are a pig!' Sandy shouted.

'Clear your books away. I want to make pastry,' Mrs Fielding said to Ian tartly. 'And you can take Gertie's lunch up when I'm ready. So don't disappear.'

'It's not my turn! It's Sandy's.'

'Sandy's been working out in the yard since seven. You haven't been out yet. Do you good.'

'It's not fair!'

'Boo-hoo!' Josie jeered. 'Sandy works like a slave. Talk about do-it-yourself. They jolly well don't, as far as I can see.'

'That's a fact,' said Mrs Fielding. 'If you're making more money, you ought to get some help for Sandy, Bill. Now the horses are all in at nights and half the owners ask Sandy to do it, it's going to be too much – nine of them.'

'Some of the owners do it,' Sandy said loyally.

'It's only Uncle Arthur who hardly ever comes, and Sneerwell is pretty hopeless, and old Stick and Ball ask me sometimes, not often. Polly and Henry never miss.'

'Duncan can lend a hand,' Bill Fielding said. 'I'll tell him.'

'Oh, no.' Sandy was shocked. Duncan the cowman worked all hours, and had to go home on a bicycle. He had horrid parents and had to give his mother nearly all his money.

'Duncan never stops. Why should he do it and not Ian?'

'A good point,' said Mary Fielding. 'Duncan has enough to do.'

'I'm not going to muck out stupid horses!' Ian shouted.

'No, but you could hump the hay and straw down from the barns,' his mother said. 'That would be a help.'

'Only if I can use the tractor.'

'I hope you'll manage to take Gertie's dinner up without using the tractor! I'm getting a bit tired of your attitude, Ian.'

Ian snatched up his books and flung out of the room.

'What's the matter with him?' Bill Fielding asked, not having noticed.

'It's his age,' said his mother.

'I thought it was only girls they say that about,' Josie said.

'People,' said Mary Fielding. 'They all have their difficult times. Ian . . . Gertie . . . '

'I hope you're not including me in that generalization,' said her husband.

She laughed. 'Oh, you! You're difficult all the time. Isn't he, Sandy?' She put her arm round Sandy and gave her a hug. 'We're the only sane ones in this house, aren't we?'

Just as she said this there was a shrill shout from outside the house. They all looked out of the window and saw Julia sitting there on Empress of China, holding a riderless King of the Fireworks by his reins.

'Oh, Lor'! What's happened?'

Sandy made a rush for the door.

Julia shouted, 'He's come off. He's unconscious! Can somebody go down?'

Sandy ran to take King of the Fireworks. 'What happened?'

'Nothing really. The horse bucked. He came off on his head. He's hopeless.'

The men came out, shrugging into their coats. 'Where is he?'

'Down by the sea-wall. Not far. On the track.'

'We'll take the Land Rover. Silly idiot!'

'That horse is much too good for him,' Julia said, slipping down from the Empress.

King of the Fireworks, undisturbed, turned his handsome head and gave Julia an affectionate shove. She patted his neck and took him into his box to unsaddle, while Sandy and Leo took the Empress. Leo noted how naturally Julia took the best horse, the star.

'It would be awful to lose Fireworks,' she said to Sandy. 'He's so lovely. What if Sneerwell's put off?'

'He can't be, or he won't get his aunt's money. I'm sure that's a terrific incentive.'

'A blow on the head might do him good.'

When they had put the horses away they all went to meet the Land Rover as it came back up the track. Mrs Fielding came out and told them to go indoors, so they waited in the kitchen while Anthony Speerwell was unloaded. He wasn't unconscious any longer, but he was extremely groggy and very cross. He refused the offer of a bed and staggered into Grandpa's easy chair by the Aga.

'Bally horse is useless!' he muttered.

Julia said in a clear voice, 'No. It's you that's useless. The horse is too good for you.'

This remark seemed to bring him round more quickly than offers of strong tea or brandy.

'What do you know about it?'

'Quite a lot, actually.'

'Don't start an argument, for goodness sake!' Mary Fielding admonished her. 'He needs to keep quiet. Just lie still, Anthony, and I'll give your mother a ring. You're in no fit state to drive yourself home.'

He groaned, but did not demur. Josie and Glynn decided to depart, and Ian took the opportunity to disappear. The three girls sat at the table and Mary Fielding gave them the potatoes to peel. Grandpa came back from the village and demanded his chair.

'You can't have it, Dad. The young man's had an accident. Sit at the table with the girls. You can read your *Sporting Life* and have a coffee.'

'Who's 'e then?' Grandpa demanded fiercely of Sandy.

Sandy explained in a soft voice and Grandpa said, 'Who? Oh, them Speerwells. She that was Nellie Pointer before she married the builder. Should 'ave known better. Money's not everything, I say.'

'Oh, shut up, Grandpa,' Sandy whispered. 'Don't be rude.'

'Rude? I'm not rude!' Grandpa trumpeted. 'I 'aven't said anything. Nellie Pointer's mother went with one of them American soldiers – what did they call them? A GI. Just when the war was ending. A bomber pilot he were and Cissie – she were called Cissie, Nellie's mother – she had a baby, that were Nellie, and folks said—'

'*Grandpa!*' Sandy could feel herself going scarlet. Leo had got the giggles.

'What you laughing for, young lady?' Grandpa demanded.

'I've just thought of a joke.'

'What's your joke then?'

'There were these pleasure boats on a lake, hired out by the hour, and the attendant shouted, "Your time's up, number ninety-nine!" and the other attendant said, "We haven't got a number ninety-nine," so then the first attendant shouted, "Are you having trouble, number sixty-six?" '

After Grandpa had worked it out he laughed so hard that he started his smoker's cough and had to be taken out into the scullery to have his back thumped and his eyes wiped. The girls got on with the potatoes, behaving themselves, until Mrs Speerwell drew up outside in her Alfa-Romeo and Mary Fielding went to greet her.

Mrs Speerwell looked about twenty-five. She was fabulously made up and dressed in a cream suede coat over a red cashmere dress, with many gold trinkets and rings. A strong smell of scent came in with her.

'Tony, darling! Whatever have you been up to?'

Sandy was pleased to see that darling Tony looked as sick as any lad whose mother was an embarrassment to him. He scowled furiously and stood up, swaying slightly, to fend her off.

'So kind of you to take him in!' Mrs Speerwell smiled. Her large blue eyes were darting about to take everything in. 'I really never know what he gets up to these days.'

'He came off his horse. I think perhaps a doctor

should check him to be on the safe side. Concussion is a tricky thing.'

'Yes, of course. I'll give Dr Menzies a ring as soon as we get home. So kind of you! Come along, Tony darling! You can walk to the car, can you?'

'Diddums,' Leo whispered.

Neither of them mentioned the horse, Sandy thought sadly, as they departed.

Grandpa came in and said, 'What's the pong in here?'

'Mrs Sneerwell,' said Leo.

'Cor. Like a funeral!' Grandpa loved funerals. They gave him a superior feeling at outdoing all these young fallers-by-the-wayside. 'What's for dinner then?'

Leo went home for her own lunch on her bicycle. Julia came with her and, after the hill flattened out, Leo let her get up behind for the ride into the village. There Leo went left and Julia right, and they parted.

Julia, walking the half-mile to her house, hugged herself with sheer joy at the glory of her day. It had been the best Saturday morning she could ever remember. It felt like six days rolled into one, and yet was only half over. Later she would go down and do Faithful for the night. She might even offer to do King of the Fireworks, too.

Leo let herself in her back door and found her

mother cutting up nuts to put in the salad. Her house was cold and silent. Her father was out birdwatching.

'Leonie, you must do something about your hair!' her mother moaned gently, as was her habit. 'You look – you look – oh dear! Dirty.'

'I am. I'm covered in horse manure. Smell me. Yum.'

Leo held her hands up close under her mother's nose. Then she picked some nuts out of the salad and ate them and her mother gave another moan. I really hate it here, Leo thought.

Sandy knew there was something wrong when they passed Gertie's house on the way to school. She stopped and Ian said, 'What's up?'

'I don't know.'

It was raining, not hard but miserably, and the water ran gurgling down the ditch in front of Gertie's house.

'I'll just give her a shout. Say hello.'

'If she starts yakking we'll miss the bus.'

'You go on then.'

Ian shrugged, scowled, and decided not to wait. Sandy cursed and went round the path to the back door. It was open. Sandy hesitated. Ian was right: the old girl had no idea about catching school buses and what it cost her, Sandy, to do this simple duty. 'I am foul,' Sandy thought, and went inside.

'Gertie!'

There was no answer.

The cat hadn't been fed and came running in after her, leaving wet paw marks over the already dirty kitchen lino. The house smelled of old woman. Sandy knew then that it was all wrong. She felt a cold hand claw at her stomach.

'Gertie!'

She would be dead in bed, Sandy thought. I can't bear it! Perhaps she should go back for her mother. She was a baby. It was all in the imagination. And to think she had sometimes toyed with the idea of being a policewoman. At least if Gertie was dead, she would be newly dead, not three weeks old like some old women who died alone. They looked after her that well, at least. But Sandy felt sick, all the same.

She went through the tiny living-room to the foot of the stairs and started up them her heart thumping. Her hands were clammy. Gertie slept in sometimes. She was imagining all this! No.

'Gertie!'

Gertie was in the bedroom, but not in bed. She lay just inside the door: her face was ghastly and there was blood everywhere.

Sandy screamed. She felt her knees give way and she fell down on the floor in a sort of stupid kneeling position. She strove to recover herself, got up and ran. She pelted down the stairs and out of the kitchen door. The rain hit her in the face, smelling of the river and the reeds and the sea. It stopped her, like a reprimand. Grow up! A policewoman! Do your duty.

She stood trembling, breathing heavily. In the

mud of the garden path at her feet, something gleamed. She picked it up. It was an old red pen-knife which she recognized – Duncan's, which he used for cutting the baler twine on the straw. She put it in her pocket. Duncan did it, she thought. Duncan wouldn't.

And then, because she had to, she went back. She climbed the stairs, breathing heavily like old Gertie herself, and forced herself to look at the old woman on the floor. She saw straightaway that she wasn't dead. Her face was bluish, but a snoring breath was flaring her nostrils at regular intervals. The blood came from the side of her head, but her skull wasn't bashed in or anything dreadful. There was a cut over her temple but the blood wasn't flowing any more but sort of hanging in congealing lumps through her mangy hair. Ugh! Sandy felt her gorge rise. She burst into tears and ran downstairs and out into the rain. She ran down the hill so fast she almost fell, shouting, 'Mummy! Mummy!' like an infant child.

Her father was coming up from the marsh meadows in the tractor, having taken feed down to the cattle. Sandy screamed at him.

'It's Gertie! Gertie's had an accident!'

'Get up here!'

He opened the door. She scrambled in and he roared up the lane to the house.

'What's happened?'

'She's lying unconscious – her head's all bleeding. Someone's hit her!'

'Hit her? More likely she just fell. Who'd hit her, for goodness sake?'

Why did she think someone had hit Gertie? Because Duncan had been there. Duncan had hit her.

'We'll get the police. And the ambulance.'

For a slow-moving man, Bill Fielding moved fast when motivated. He went indoors to the phone and Sandy followed him, shivering. Then her mother ran out and said, 'Sandy, are you all right? Darling!' She put her arms round her in a brief hug and gave her a sharp look.

'I'll have to go up there. But you stay here. Make yourself some strong sweet tea – you know, like the books say!' and she was gone.

Sandy went indoors and it was very quiet. She felt stone cold and went and wedged herself against the Aga. The breakfast things were still on the table. Ian would be mad at missing the excitement! Serve him right! She had been noble, her caring nature going to look, and she had saved Gertie's life. Or might have. Her mother wouldn't have gone up till lunchtime, by which time Gertie was bound to have died. How long had she been lying there? Since last night, or had it happened early in the morning? What a tough old bird!

She dithered about for a bit, then cleared the

breakfast things and put the kettle on. She was all shaky and her mind kept shooting about. She couldn't think straight about anything.

Her mother came back in about an hour. She had a policeman with her.

'He just wants to ask you a few questions, Sandy, about how you found her. The ambulance has taken her away and they think she'll be all right.'

The policeman was young and friendly. He sat at the table and Mary Fielding made more tea, and Sandy explained how she had gone in, just to say hello, and found Gertie in her bedroom.

'You didn't touch her at all? You didn't move anything?'

'No. I just screamed and ran.'

'Was the back door open or shut? How did you get in?'

'It was open. But she often leaves it open, even in the winter, for the cat. She gets up early. I wasn't surprised it was open.'

She remembered Duncan's penknife lying on the path. She wouldn't mention it.

'Did someone do it? Or did she just fall?' she asked.

'We can't tell. You didn't notice anything different from usual? Do you usually call in?'

'No, I didn't notice anything. I quite often call in. Not always.'

She wasn't going to say about her gut feeling

that something had been wrong. There was no way to describe that.

'That's all for now. I've no doubt the inspector will want to ask you some more questions later, Mrs Fielding. About who might have been in the vicinity last night, that sort of thing.'

He drank his tea and departed.

'Oh dear.' Mary Fielding looked at Sandy sadly. 'It's a bad business. Her savings are all gone. You know she keeps an envelope full of ten-pound notes under her mattress? I told them, and they looked, and it's not there.'

'Everybody knows that. Everyone in the village,' Sandy said. 'She tells everyone it's safer than in a bank. And who does he mean, everyone in the vicinity? All of us? Last night?'

It was a Monday morning, a week after Sneerwell had fallen off King of the Fireworks.

'Everyone was here last night. Sunday night,' Sandy said. 'Sneerwell, Leo, Julia, Polly, Henry, Stick and Ball – even Uncle Arthur came down last night.'

'That boy on the grey went past in the dark, flat gallop as usual. Glynn came down with the new gate.'

'Dad and Ian, you and me!' And Duncan, Sandy thought. But didn't say. 'Grandpa!'

'Grandpa was the last to see her. He called in at teatime. He'll get a shock when he hears!'

'Where is he?'

87

'He's moving the electric fence in the top field.'

'But anyone could have done it!'

'Yes, of course. Anyone from the village. Or a stranger. The mattress isn't a very original place to keep cash, after all.' Mrs Fielding looked rather old suddenly, Sandy thought. 'Poor Gertie – oh, poor Gertie! What a terrible thing to have happened to her! It can't be anyone we know. They said she must have been lying there all night. Poor old soul!'

'She might have fought back. She would, I think.'

'She's certainly a fearless woman. But this will do her so much harm, mentally. She won't be able to live on her own after this.'

'She'd never go in a home!'

'No. Imagine! She'd drive them all mad. I don't know what will happen.' Mary Fielding slumped, in the old-looking way, and said nothing for a few moments, then she visibly pulled herself together and said briskly, 'Well, I shall go along to the hospital and see how she's doing, and I'll take you to school on the way. It's no good sitting here thinking about it. That'll get us nowhere.'

Sandy felt the day was half over, but she was as yet only half an hour late for school. Amazing. When she went in, in the middle of a lesson, and explained why she was late, she became the centre of attention all day and everyone wanted to hear the story of her going upstairs and finding the blood-covered old lady. She was almost a heroine, as if she had done something clever. She was ashamed of how she had reacted, but didn't tell anyone that. Ian guessed. He said, nastily, 'I bet you passed out, came to half an hour later and ran for Mummy.'

'What would you have done, Bighead?'

On the bus, going home, Leo said, 'Are we all under suspicion then? We were all there last night.'

'It was dark when I left,' Julia said. 'The light was on in her kitchen. She must have been OK then.'

Julia was turning round from the seat in front. So far she had been quite bearable and Sandy and Leo had cautiously let her into their friendship – the part of it that was to do with the horses. She came down night and morning, devotedly, and helped around quite a lot. Sandy found her very useful and was impressed (without remarking on it) by her vast knowledge of The Horse, Its Ways and How to Look After It. Only Polly Marlin equalled her in this. She too had been there last night, late. Polly was famously, perennially, hard up, spending her every penny on her eventer, Charlie's Flying. So was Sneerwell, apart from his fast car. Daddy Sneerwell kept him on a tight rein, so that he wouldn't do anything silly. But if he got King of the Fireworks round a team-chase he was going to come into money. Stealing

Gertie's savings would be much quicker. And Duncan, Duncan of the Penknife, gave all his money to his grasping mother . . .

Sandy's mind flew round like a Catherine wheel, shooting sparks and getting nowhere. She was frightened by how suddenly a threat had come into their dozy domestic life.

'It's bound to be somebody we don't know, a tramp or something. Anyone could come down the lane.'

'Or up the river from a boat!'

'It's Ian,' Leo said mischievously. 'That's why he wouldn't go in.'

'Oh, great!' said Ian. 'I reckon it's Dad. He's going bankrupt fast.'

'Shut up!' snapped Sandy, because she knew it was true.

Julia got off the bus. She always went home for her tea and came down later on her bike. It was too dark to ride after school now, and Faithful was turned out by day, as were most of the horses.

'It's her,' Leo said. 'She was telling me she had no idea how she was going to pay her livery soon as she's nearly used up all her savings.'

'It's your dad,' Ian said to her. 'He's a psychopath.'

'He's pretty weird,' Leo agreed equably.

'Mummy Marsden has said she'll have Faithful home after all. She's got over her paddy. But Julia doesn't want to go.' Sandy had heard this from

Julia herself and nurtured the thought with some pride: that her stable could be more attractive to Julia than her own home. 'She likes us.'

'I always thought she was unbalanced,' Ian said.

'Why is he so horrible?' Leo asked as Ian moved seats to talk to someone else.

'Mum says it's his age.'

'It's taking a long time, his age. I think it's permanent,' Leo said.

'Some people are naturally horrid, I suppose.' Sandy then mentioned what had been in her head for some time: 'The wild boy came up the lane late last night. The police will have to know that. We might find out about him.'

'What if he stole the money?'

'Yes, I wondered. Oh, I hope not!'

'When you think of it, there are dozens of possibilities! It's like an Agatha Christie.' As Sandy stood up to get off the bus, Leo added, 'I'll say it wasn't you. I was with you all the time.'

When Sandy and Ian walked home down their lane in the dusk, they found Gertie's cottage surrounded by markers of red-and-white tape. Two police cars were parked outside and the lights were all on. They walked by. Sandy found herself feeling shaky again and a bit sick.

'She might've died by now,' Ian said.

But when they got home their mother said Gertie was all right. Conscious. She wasn't sure what had happened to her. She thought she had heard someone upstairs and remembered going up.

'It were that slippery mat done for me.'

'The police are coming down about six, when most of the livery people will be here, to ask if anyone remembers seeing anything useful. And they want the name of the boy on the grey horse. You said you knew who he was, Ian. They want you to tell them.'

Sandy put her hand in her pocket and her fingers closed round the red penknife. When they asked her if she had found anything, would she say?

'You'd better get your tea early,' their mother said.

Sandy ate her tea and went out to the yard. Duncan was there, unloading straw from the tractor trailer. Sandy went over to help, out of habit, and found herself tongue-tied. She wanted to mention the penknife, but found the words wouldn't come. She had always liked Duncan; he was more like a brother than Ian, and much nicer. He had worked on the farm ever since she could remember, coming down as a boy to help in his spare time before he had been employed. He loved the farm and the cattle and the work and would have given anything to be in Ian's shoes, taking over from his father. Sandy was convinced Ian never would take over, he hated it so.

'You will have it, you're the only one,' she had told Duncan.

'But I can never own it! If it can't be passed into the family, your father will sell it.'

'He can pass it on to me. I wouldn't mind being a farmer,' Sandy said. After this conversation she realized the brilliant thing would be for her and Duncan to get married. This thought embarrassed her so much that she now found it difficult to talk to him easily. She wondered if the same thought had passed through his mind. If it had, he made no sign.

He threw the bales down off the trailer and she stacked them until they got too high. Then he came to do it. He was enormously strong from so much outdoor work, but was gentle by nature, which made him a very good cowman. He was seventeen, like Ian, but very responsible. He had a quiet voice and manner, yet no-one took advantage of him; Bill Fielding never shouted at him, like he did at Ian.

'It's a bad do about Gertie,' he said. 'Must have given you a fright, finding her.'

'Yes.' She hoicked a bale towards him. 'The police are coming down to ask questions.'

'Why's that then?'

'Her money's been stolen. All that money in her mattress.'

Duncan stopped, in mid-fling, and looked down from the stack, shocked. Sandy tried to notice if it was play-acting, but it was difficult in the half-light.

'Who'd do a thing like that?'

Exactly. Stealing from an old girl like Gertie was too awful. There was no way she could mention the penknife. He would think she was accusing him.

He went home after stacking the straw, and the livery people started to dribble in to hear the news. There was no sign of Sneerwell, as usual, so Sandy got a headcollar and went down to catch King of the Fireworks out of the field, with Polly and Henry. They were going to ride, although it was nearly dark. They schooled in the field just down from the yard, which was flat and gravelly and didn't get too poached.

'The police are coming.'

'They think it's one of us!'

Sandy put Sneerwell's horse in its box, changed its rug and went back to Polly, who said she had her livery money to give her.

'I had it in my pocket last week,' she said. 'But when I came to give it you, it was gone. I blamed my own carelessness, but if there's a crook like that around – who knows?' She passed Sandy a twenty-pound note. 'Perhaps someone pinched it.'

Sandy was horrified. 'Don't say that!'

'I never thought it before. But now . . . I left my jacket in the tackroom. Anyone could've done it.'

Polly was a blunt, down-to-earth female in her early twenties. What Ian called a 'real horsy woman'. She was a very hard worker and tough, but easy enough to get on with, and Sandy depended quite a lot on her knowledge and expertise. She really knew horses and thought of little else. Her horse was a dark grey, rather funny-looking ex-racehorse called Charlie's Flying. Although he had rather a lot wrong with him, he was a good jumper and fast, and the best Polly could afford. She loved competing on him, but rarely won anything. Polly worked in the local supermarket. She was quite pretty when she made an effort, which was rarely, but her shrewd eyes and hard manner put the men off. Sandy liked her a lot and thought she looked marvellous on her horse in her competition gear – like a being from another planet. Sometimes Sandy went to events with her, to help, and she was always impressed by the way Polly got Charlie's Flying round the cross-country course – no easy option.

She hung over the stable door, while Polly gave her horse a quick brush over and put on the saddle and bridle.

'Will you tell the police about your money?'

'If they ask, I suppose. Mind you don't lose it!'

Sandy put the note in the zip pocket of her jods. Nobody would take it from there.

'Is our friend Sneerwell coming down tonight?'

Polly asked. 'That horse is tragically wasted on that young man. I'll give him lessons, if he wants.'

'He doesn't think he needs them.'

Polly gave a snort of derision. 'Poor deluded soul.'

She led Charlie's Flying out of his box and hopped up into the saddle, quick as a sparrow. Charlie's faults: too long a back, sloping rump, dishing action, cow hocks, bowed tendons – all seemed to disappear when his rider collected him up and sent him on at a perfectly collected trot. Polly was an ace rider.

Sandy felt gloomy, fingering the twenty-pound note that nestled in her groin. Polly's information was bad news. She would have to tell her parents.

She went to fetch George and Puffin, who now came in at night. They were waiting by the gate, and Leo came down on her bicycle to coincide with Sandy in the gateway. They led the ponies with baler twine; they would have come home without anything. Leo rode her bike and held Puffin's mane, and Puffin pulled her along. Sandy told Leo about Polly's twenty-pound note disappearing. 'But don't tell anyone else!' She wasn't going to tell Leo about Duncan's penknife. Not anybody.

George and Puffin seemed to get smaller and smaller. After handling King of the Fireworks the contrast was marked. Or were they – their riders – growing? Panic seized Sandy when she thought of being too big for George. Her father would never buy her another, not when he couldn't even afford a new baling machine.

'Anyway, George, I don't want another one. Only you. Why can't you grow too?'

George was only interested in his feed bucket. Sandy knew he wasn't anything special, but she loved him. He was a goer and a fun ride and hardy: he never got tired. Polly said he should pull a cart. His markings were good – more brown than white, evenly distributed, and he had a pretty head and good eyes – a touch of quality, Sandy liked to think. Everyone thought their pigs were pearls. She wasn't the only one. Only Sneerwell, who had a peerless horse, didn't think he had anything special. He was pig ignorant and couldn't see a pearl when it was under his nose. Sandy fed Sneerwell's pearl as its owner appeared, as usual, not to be coming.

By the time she had done this the two police cars had arrived in the front drive. Sandy came out of Fireworks' stable and, as she did so, Julia rode in on Faithful (having been for a smart canter in the dusk) and said, 'The wild boy is coming along the sea-wall, if the police want to see him. Shall I tell them?'

Without waiting for an answer she rode through the archway into the drive and approached the policemen, who were talking beside their cars. One of the policemen got back into his car and drove it out down the drive and into the lane, blocking it. This movement looked very threatening, Sandy thought, although she could see it was perfectly practical. Literally 'stopped by the police'. She and Leo wanted to hang around to witness the taming of the wild boy but without making it obvious. It was a bit tricky. Then one of the policemen came over to Sandy and asked her if she could let 'the liveries' know they would like to ask them if they had seen anything untoward the evening before. Was there a room they could use, to take notes?

'You can use the tackroom. There's a table and chairs.'

'That will be fine. Thank you.'

Leo then said, cleverly, 'Shall we stop the boy on the grey horse and tell him you want to speak to him?'

'That would be very helpful. Then we needn't wait up there.'

Sandy and Leo scampered down the driveway to the junction with the lane and peered through the dusk in the direction of the sea-wall. They were just in time, for the boy was coming up at his usual gallop. Fortunately, he could see the police car blocking his way and started to pull up before he reached the girls. Even with only a halter for control, he had the horse perfectly in hand and it pulled up as if it were in a dressage arena, dropping its nose obediently.

'What's the game?'

The boy looked down on the girls angrily, even defiantly. He did not look scared or guilty, they noticed, only annoyed. At close quarters he seemed to be about sixteen, slenderly built and certainly gypsy-looking, with tousled black hair and frowning dark eyes. He had high cheekbones and a hawkish nose and an undoubted air of superb self-confidence, bordering on arrogance. Although it was quite cold he wore only a dark T-shirt and faded jeans.

Leo stepped forward and said boldly, 'The police are questioning all the people who were down here yesterday evening – all of us, that is. And you were too. The old lady who lives in the cottage up there was robbed of all her savings.'

'I didn't do it!'

'No. It's only routine questions, in case you saw anything.'

'I didn't see anything either.'

'No. You have to tell them though. Your name and all that.'

'I'm in a hurry.'

'You're always in a hurry.'

The boy hesitated and looked at Leo more closely. 'What's it got to do with you?'

'Nothing. We just said we'd stop you, that's all. To help them – the police. If you ride on, they'll probably think you're guilty.'

'Where are they then?'

'In the stable-yard.'

The boy stared at the police car and hesitated some more, then he saw the sense of Leo's argument and shrugged. The girls started back for the yard and he followed. His grey horse, from being all fire, was now as mild as milk, not tizzed up like most horses after a gallop, but gentle and quiet. At close quarters the grey, a mare, was beautiful; Sandy was entranced with her. She had enormous dark eyes like her owner and a fine silver mane. She was lightly built but very compact, about fifteen hands, and she moved like a dream. She was slightly too thin, no doubt with all the galloping, but the loveliest horse Sandy thought she had ever seen.

They went into the yard and one of the policemen was standing in the doorway of the tackroom. The boy rode over and pulled up beside him. The policeman asked him to dismount. He slipped off with one agile movement.

'What is your name, sir?' the policeman asked.

'Jonas Brown.'

Sandy and Leo knew they couldn't stand there gawping, so retreated into George's loosebox and sat in the straw.

'Jonas! What a gorgeous name! Isn't he heavenly!'

'And the horse, the mare! She's a dream horse!'

'You don't think he did it, do you?'

'Of course not!'

'You ought to get them here – as liveries!

Wouldn't it be wonderful? That boy – he's fantastic!'

'The Magic Man?' Sandy enquired.

'Oh yes!'

'I think the horse is magic.'

Julia went past, saw them and came in.

'Who's that boy then?'

'Jonas Brown.'

'Oh, *him*. Is that who he is? Fancy.'

'What do you mean? Do you know him?'

'Yes,' said Julia. 'He used to show-jump when he was little. I didn't recognize him on the sea-wall.'

'Where does he come from?'

'His father's a fisherman from Riverhead. A very rough man. His mother left, that's why he didn't come show-jumping any more. She was the horsy one. She taught him.'

Sandy and Leo digested this in silence. Trust Julia to know! She would no doubt take him over, as she had taken over Sneerwell. She seemed to have no inhibitions when it came to barging in.

'He could've done it. His father's not very honest. Got done for pinching a horsebox once,' Julia said coolly.

'How could he have done it, with the horse?' Sandy demanded hotly.

'It stands when he asks it. I've seen. Down on the sea-wall once, he got off to go out to a boat – a yachtsman he knew wanted some help to get his engine started or something – and it just stood there, not even tied up. Didn't graze or anything. Like in a cowboy film.'

Sandy looked out and saw that the mare was standing now. Jonas was in the tackroom. She leaned her chin on the half-door, disturbed. All these things – first Duncan, then Polly saying she had lost the twenty-pound note, and now the wild boy – her solid world was beginning to revolve.

She slipped out, leaving Leo and Julia, and went over to the mare. The mare put her soft muzzle in Sandy's hand and gave her a friendly shove. All she had for a bridle was a piece of rope knotted over her ears and round her nose – nothing through her mouth. Her grey coat was pale in the dusk, ghostlike; she would soon be pure white.

While she was standing there, Jonas came out.

Sandy said, 'What's your horse's name?'

'Queen Moon.'

'She's lovely. I wish you kept her here.'

The boy looked at her, not crossly but apparently interested.

'I haven't got anywhere to keep her. Only a shed.'

'You could come here!'

He shrugged. 'Costs money.' He mounted with one easy hop. 'I haven't got any.'

'It's very cheap here. I'd look after her for you.' She hadn't meant to say this, it just slipped out.

She felt almost desperate to see more of this lovely mare.

The boy was riding out of the yard. He half pulled up, looked down on Sandy, and actually smiled.

'I'll bear it in mind.'

His smile showed teeth as white as his mare's mane, shining in his gypsy face. Sandy felt her heart turn over. The Magic Man indeed! But she would never admit it to Leo, never. Leo made a joke of everything. Sandy felt that something very serious had happened, meeting Jonas Brown and his mare Queen Moon.

'We really must do something about it,' Polly said to Sandy. 'He'll ruin that horse if he goes on like this.'

Sneerwell was riding King of the Fireworks in the schooling field, trying to make him jump. The big horse did not know what was required, as every time he set off towards a jump, Sneerwell, in his nervousness, pulled hard on his mouth, restraining him. Sneerwell called it 'steadying for the approach'. He had read it in books.

'Do teach him!' Sandy pleaded. She couldn't bear it either. 'He must realize by now that he's getting nowhere!'

It was gone Christmas. The year had so far been surprisingly mild and dry and sometimes, already, Sandy thought she could smell spring. The days were slowly drawing out.

Polly and Sandy leaned on the paddock rails and watched Sneerwell steer for a pair of low rails set on blocks. He had a good natural balance and plenty of enthusiasm, but no sensitivity at all. King of the Fireworks was a highly schooled horse and could not make head or tail of what was expected of him. He refused and showed his disapproval by bucking.

'Old boot, you!' Sneerwell shouted.

He rode across and said to them, 'Honestly, this horse is useless. You saw him there. What am I supposed to do with him?'

Polly straightened up and said purposefully, 'Do you really want to know, Mr Speerwell?'

He looked rather surprised, glaring down. How handsome he was, Sandy thought, his colour raised and his bright blue eyes sparkling with annoyance! What a pity he was such a nerd.

'Tell me, Miss Marlow,' he said sarcastically.

'Miss Mar*lin*,' Polly corrected him. 'As in spike.'

He grinned. 'Very appropriate.'

'Yes. What you should do,' Polly said very pointedly, speaking as if to an infant, 'is learn to ride properly.'

'Like you, I suppose?' he said insolently.

'Yes.'

There was a long silence. They stared at each other. Sandy could sense decisions being taken, and realized, with both amazement and relief, that Sneerwell was actually digesting Polly's criticism. His thick, thick skin was showing cracks. It had taken long enough.

'Four months you've had that horse, and you

haven't yet jumped it successfully in the paddock, let alone across country. Even Sandy here could get him over these schooling jumps.'

Afterwards, Sandy felt somewhat grieved about the 'even Sandy', but at the time she was too pop-eyed at the course the conversation was taking. Sneerwell slumped in his saddle and looked quite pathetic.

'Get off,' Polly said.

He obeyed. Polly climbed the fence, hopped up on King of the Fireworks and shortened her stirrups. She had never ridden him before. Sandy saw the horse come together in his lovely noble fashion, prick his ears and paw the ground to go. Polly rode him away at a lovely gliding trot, beautifully on the bit, light as a feather. After three circuits she turned him towards the rails that Sneerwell had been trying to jump and popped him over without any effort or fuss. He never once looked like jibbing or refusing, and jumped with a lovely arch and obvious pleasure. Polly rode back to the fence.

'Your aunt knew what she was doing. This horse is an absolute saint. They come like this once in a blue moon. You, even you, Anthony Speerwell, could learn to ride this horse cross-country if you take lessons.'

'From you, I suppose? Well, I do need the money,' he said. 'I really do.'

'What's this deal then? Your aunt left you

something in her will if you got round a team-chase course?'

'She left me the horse. This on the strength of my staying with her a few times when I was little. She got me a pony and I used to gallop about and she said she hoped I would be a great horseman. Then I didn't see her for years, did I? And she died. I got this horse delivered to me along with a great spiel from her solicitor, saying that she wanted me to carry on the horse tradition in the family and if I took King of the Fireworks team-chasing successfully then that would be proof that I was worth her faith in me and she would leave me all the family silver. This is worth about seventy thousand quid apparently. My parents say she's raving mad, but the solicitor says it's a perfectly legal and watertight arrangement. I have three years in which to do it.'

'Have you got to win? How many have you got to win?'

'No. Just be in a team, she said, and complete the course. Five times.'

Polly's eyes gleamed. 'Why didn't you say all this before? Of course you can do it! If you *learn*, that is! Heavens above, Tony Speerwell, what an offer! You can't fail with a horse like Fireworks! We've got the makings of a team from this stable – you and me and Julia – we only want one more . . . If you really want this, you can't fail!'

'I thought it would be easy, but—'

'Why the hell didn't you say all this weeks ago, instead of poncing about telling everyone you could ride?'

'I can ride!'

'Rubbish. You're hopeless. But I'll teach you, if you want. I'll teach you to ride!'

Polly positively vibrated with excitement. Sandy watched the two of them, fascinated by seeing Polly's will acting on Speerwell's arrogance. His realization at last that he needed help to win his fortune was very hard for him to accept. The struggle showed as he glared at Polly. Nobody had told him to his face that he was hopeless before.

'Look, if you want it, you'll learn,' Polly said. 'But only if you accept right at the start that you don't know anything. The only thing you've got going for you is good natural balance, and that is a very good bonus. Apart from that, you're hopeless. You've got to acknowledge it.'

'If I can't ride, how do I know you can teach?'

'You take my word for it. If I can't get you jumping round this paddock by the end of the month, I'll – I'll—' Words failed her. 'I just will. You can start now, if you like.'

A long, long silence.

Then, 'All right,' said Anthony Speerwell.

'I don't believe it!' said Leo.

'It's true. I was there. I saw it happen.'

'And Polly said we could make a team from here?'

'She said her and Fireworks and Julia and one other.'

'Who's the one other?'

Sandy had rather wondered that.

Leo said, 'Empress of China would do it if she had the right rider.'

They both rode Empress of China. Sandy didn't say anything, but noticed that Leo looked suspiciously vacant. Did she have ambitions? They were both growing out of their ponies fast.

'Julia could ride Empress,' she said. 'Faithful's too small for team-chasing.'

'Faithful can jump anything.'

'Team-chasers have to be fourteen two.'

'Perhaps Jonas would come!'

They went into a trance, gazing into the distance. Jonas now acknowledged them when they met – a quick nod of the head, no words, no smile. He hadn't been arrested for stealing Gertie's money. No-one had. The police had found no clues to go on.

'She's coming home tomorrow.'

Gertie was coming to stay at Drakesend until she felt fit to go back to her cottage. Against her better judgement, Mary Fielding had offered the old girl a home. Sandy and Ian dreaded it, and Sandy felt bad about dreading it, but it made no difference – she just did. She thought her mother and father rather dreaded it too, but they didn't admit to it. Grandpa drove them potty at times but he was their own and they were used to him, whereas Gertie . . . she wasn't a quiet, smiling old thing sitting in a corner knitting, but a shrewish, waspish, talkative, fidgety, gossipy old bore.

Nobody could quite foresee how Grandpa would take it. The two of them! Sandy groaned. She still worried about Duncan and the penknife and not telling anybody, and about the fact that she had lost – lost? – another thirty pounds that Stick and Ball had given her for their rent. She had put it in her anorak pocket and hung her anorak in the tackroom while she groomed King of the Fireworks. In the evening when she had looked for the money it had gone. People had been in and out all the evening, as usual; the pocket was zipped up and the money couldn't have fallen out. She hadn't told anyone this time, except Leo, and her father thought she had used the money to buy feed – he was a bit lax about her accounts and left her to make her own 'money-book'. For some reason she could not explain, she did not want to tell her parents. She was frightened of who it might be, afraid that she might be badly hurt in the discovery. Her world was close and good, and she didn't want anything spoiled. But the loss haunted her.

'It was my fault. I should have put it in my jods. But I never thought it would happen again.'

'We'll have to set a trap,' Leo said, 'and watch.' She was vague as to the details.

'Do you think it's the same person that pinched Gertie's money?'

'Yes,' said Leo.

'That was wicked.'

'So is taking money from someone who trusts you.'

Sandy did not want to think about it. It was very nasty. If anything happened again, she would have to tell her parents. But her livery venture was a success so far, one of the few successes around lately, and she did not want to add to her father's woes. He was proud of the stable and told everyone how hard she worked and what a good little businesswoman she was. It was nice to be respected. If Anthony Speerwell was really going to turn over a new leaf that would be a great bonus, and if they made up a team from the stable . . . who could tell where success would take them? Everyone needed dreams.

The next day Gertie came home.

She appropriated Grandpa's chair beside the kitchen fire and started a long rambling diatribe about life in hospital. She said the same things over and over again. Grandpa came in and wanted his chair, but Mary Fielding tactfully deflected him into Bill's chair and said she would bring Gertie's own chair up from her cottage tomorrow and he could have his chair back then. The only good thing about Gertie was that she was now sparkling clean and smelled of soap and talcum powder – a great improvement.

'That bang on the 'ead not done 'er any good as far as I can see,' Grandpa said loudly. 'Take more than that to shut 'er up.'

'Hush, Dad. That's not kind.'

'I never said she could 'ave my chair.'

'Just for tonight.'

After supper, Gertie wanted a game show on television. Ian wanted his favourite sports report. Grandpa got his chair back by moving smartly from the supper table, and Gertie said the Fieldings had never had any manners and she remembered when old Herbert Fielding had farted in church during the Easter communion. Grandpa said she was a one to talk: he could remember her dropping her drawers to show the boys at a halfpenny a time behind the school coalshed—

'Oh, shut up!' Mary Fielding hissed furiously, crashing the dishes into the sink. She turned the television up.

Ian ran out of the kitchen, slamming the door behind him. Sandy followed him and found him in the sitting-room which was only used at Christmas, huddled over the faintly warm storage heater. It was dark and she had a terrible shock when she saw that he was crying.

'I can't stand this place! I can't stand it!'

Sandy, for once, could not find it in her heart to criticize him. She stared out of the uncurtained window, pretending she hadn't noticed his tears, and said blankly, 'It'll improve. Mum'll sort it out. It's only until she's better enough to go back to her cottage.'

'Grandpa's just as bad!'

'You mustn't take any notice.'

It was true that Grandpa was always telling Ian how young boys today had it made, were molly-coddled . . . 'When I was lad I was out to work when I was eleven, hoeing turnips.' Grandpa didn't think a boy should work at his books. Cissy stuff. But Ian was strangely uptight these days. Sandy had a sudden horrendous thought that *he* might have taken her thirty pounds. He had come in the yard that night, she remembered suddenly, to get some binder twine. She felt all her insides go cold. She could not take this! Not after thinking about Duncan too.

'I've had thirty pounds stolen, out of the tack-room. My livery money. I haven't told Mum and Dad, but I don't know what to do.' She turned round and faced him. Neither of them had put the light on, but the room was filled with the cold moonlight of the February night. She saw Ian lift his head up from the storage heater.

'You should tell them,' he said.

She felt better then.

'It's horrible. You suspect everyone. After Gertie as well.'

He shrugged. 'Everyone I know is short of cash. If you leave it lying about, what do you expect?'

Sandy was shocked. 'Why? You wouldn't, would you?'

'No. I wouldn't. But I know a lot that would.'

Who, Sandy wondered? But the icy fear of suspecting Ian had left her. How foul it was that this person's offence polluted normal thinking – that she could have sprung to such a suspicion!

'It's hateful when you feel it must be someone you know.'

Ian blew his nose, his self-pity deflected.

Sandy switched the subject. 'I suppose we could come here, away from *them*, if we light a fire.'

'There's no telly in here.'

'Perhaps we could get one of our own.' Julia Marsden had her own in her bedroom, Sandy remembered.

It was a long time since she had spoken agreeably with Ian. He did have problems, she supposed. More than she did.

'I'll ask Julia if she's got a spare. They seem to have two of everything at hers. Dishwasher, jacuzzi, yard-sweeper, electric groomer – she's got her own video recorder as well as TV.'

'I can't think why she keeps her pony here.'

'She likes us!' Julia was getting too friendly

with Leo, and had a crush on Anthony Speerwell. Sandy could never work out how well she liked her. She was a prickly girl, quick to take offence, but she worked hard and helped.

The house was freezing in February, but Mary Fielding agreed that to keep the peace there should be two living-rooms. The tractor was despatched up to the woods to bring home fallen timber for the sitting-room fire. She bought a portable television in a jumble sale and gave it to Ian. It had a ten-inch screen, but he didn't complain. Grandpa and Gertie sat on in the kitchen, arguing and shouting at each other or else silently digesting soap opera and late-night sex discussions. Bill and Mary Fielding, divorced from the television, took up reading and tapestry respectively and found that they enjoyed their evenings more. Bill usually fell asleep, whatever he was doing.

By the end of the month Polly had taught Tony – now that he had come to heel he was called Tony instead of Sneerwell – to get King of the Fireworks round the little jumping course in the schooling field. She had taught him to sit properly, use his hands properly, go forward with the horse and leave the horse's head free over the jump. Because he was ambitious and reasonably talented, Tony learned fast. It was hard for him to accept Polly's rather abrasive teaching in spite of his determination, for his natural arrogance kept bobbing up, but after two or three weeks they had come to terms with each other. Tony's pride became a lever for Polly, her derision steeling him to 'show her'.

'It's unbelievable – the improvement.' Julia was impressed. 'He really will be able to do a hunter trials in the spring at this rate. Perhaps I'll take Faithful, too.'

The competition fever was infectious: Sandy longed to have a pony that would do cross-country. George wasn't a bad jumper but he stopped dead at anything he didn't like the look of. He was very sensible. He hated water and ditches. And even his fastest gallop put him on the limit of 'time allowed'. Besides which, Sandy's heels came almost down to his knees.

'I want a new pony,' she whispered to her mother.

'Bad luck, Sandy,' said her mother gently. 'No go, I'm afraid, at the moment.'

As Uncle Arthur still wanted Empress of China exercised, both Sandy and Leo took it in turns to ride her. Fitter now, she was an easy ride and they both got to like the feel of a big horse. In spite of the fact that she was a funny-looking creature, she had good paces. But when she took a hold along the bottom pastures she could frighten them both with her thoroughbred power. They weighed nothing compared with Uncle Arthur and she thought she was a racehorse again with a little seven-stone lad astride. She dropped ten years and her dull old eyes glittered.

'We've got our team,' Polly exclaimed, watching. 'Charlie's Flying, King of the Fireworks, Empress of China and Faithful.'

She carefully did not say who was to ride Empress of China.

'What about Faithful being too small?'

'Oh, we'll get her shod with pads. Stand her on uneven ground when she's measured. Something. It's only an inch. No-one'll object.' Horse people, fierce competitors, were notorious at bending rules. 'It's not as if she's got any form.'

'She can certainly jump.'

'She's never done team-chasing.'

Tony Speerwell, finding approbation, seemed to grow nicer. He was coming up to his nineteenth birthday and was going to have a party. He gave them all invitations.

'Bring your boyfriends,' he said kindly.

They went scarlet.

'We haven't got any,' said Leo bitterly, when they were alone. 'Do you think Ian'd come if I asked him?'

Sandy had been wondering about Duncan. But it was too embarrassing. She went into a dream about meeting Jonas and him saying how lovely she was and agreeing to take her to Speerwell's party.

'I don't know,' she said. It answered everything in her life. She felt deeply depressed. Since Gertie had come, home wasn't as nice any more. Her mother had become irritable and over-pressed, keeping the peace between warring factions. Sometimes Gertie and Grandpa seemed to have taken over completely, turning a united front against the rest of them while they commandeered the fire and the best chairs and the television. Even the dogs left them and joined the family in the sitting-room.

'Roll on summer,' Mary said hopefully.

'She'll go then, won't she?'

'I'm working on it.'

On Saturday morning, Sandy rode over to visit Josie. She thought Josie might be good for her. Josie and Glynn were always short of money: perhaps they would take Gertie? Gertie gave all her pension money to her hosts and, in fact, ate very little. It must be profitable. Sandy knew her mother didn't do it for the money but because she was kind, but other people might do it for the money.

It was a cheerful day, the sun slanting brightly across the marshes and the wild ducks mating noisily on the river. George went with gusto and Sandy forgot about what she didn't have and decided that what she did have wasn't bad at all. Moods swung for no reason. There was no cause for her to feel miserable. She could ask Josie what she should do about her missing thirty pounds. Josie always had an answer for everything. Her whole life had appeared to be in ruins when she got pregnant, but she had weathered the storm like a lifeboat. Josie never went under.

Sandy had hoped she might meet Jonas, but she didn't. However, when she left the sea-wall and turned up the track that led to the Elizabethan tower, she saw Queen Moon grazing at the side of Josie's garden. Her rope halter was tied round her neck, but she was loose. When she saw George she lifted her head and gave a soft whinny.

'Whatever are you doing here?'

Sandy pulled up and stared at her. She was a dream horse, shining like a silvery ghost in the shadows under the gnarled oaks; she was so fine and delicate compared with George. Yet Sandy knew she was as hard as nails. She had long, shapely ears and her forelock blew up in the morning breeze as she turned her head.

'Oh, you are so beautiful!'

To Sandy at that moment, Queen Moon was the essence of the unattainable; Queen Moon was perfection. Queen Moon was all her dreams rolled into one tangible thing, standing there looking at her with her huge, kind eyes. George stopped and gave a snort.

'Oh, get on, pig,' Sandy said, snappishly.

Then she was sorry and gave him a pat, and he walked past Queen Moon to the gate of Josie's garden. Sandy slipped off. She suddenly realized that Jonas might be visiting. Did he know Josie? Why else was Queen Moon there?

'He's gone with Glynn to give him a hand with some timber. Two-man job. Glynn met him down by the river and they got talking. Now he comes up to help sometimes,' Josie explained.

Sandy, having tied George up inside the fence, sat in Josie's kitchen. It was the bottom room in the tower, round in shape like a lighthouse, with a stone staircase running up one wall to disappear through a hole in the ceiling. The ceiling was very high. Glynn had fixed a stove against the wall opposite the door, which had a wire-netting fence round it to keep the now crawling baby at bay, and there was a large table in the middle and a long sofa to sprawl on, colourful rag mats on the stone floor and a great forest of greenery growing out of pots. It didn't look like anyone else's kitchen that Sandy knew. The windows were made of Tudor glass in tiny leaded squares and gave a yellow, squinting view of the outside, so that nothing looked quite real. No wonder Josie was happy. Sandy wished she came more often: it was enchanting. But the livery yard took all her spare time.

'Here, have a biscuit.' Josie took a great tray of shortbread out of her Calor gas oven. She was

always cooking or sewing or potting or pro-
ducing something – a very creative girl. She never
stopped. She flashed Sandy her quick, dark smile.
She wore red dungarees and a navy shirt and her
hair was a black cloud round her head. No wonder
she had been snapped up before she was twenty.
She was very like Ian in looks, Sandy noticed
suddenly: they were both like their mother. She
was like her father who was fair and paunchy. Just
her luck.

The baby, Selina, was biting the toe of her
boot.

'It's been in the muck-heap, Selina.' Sandy
picked the baby up. It felt boneless and warm
and cuddly. She wasn't very good at holding it.
It had a great loony smile with one tooth inside
it and buttercup-yellow hair. It too was like its
father.

'Sneerwell's asked us to his party. Bring a boy,
he said. And I haven't got one.'

'You can have Glynn if you like.'

'He's too old.'

'I thought you hated Sneerwell.'

Sandy explained about his turning nicer.

'They give wonderful parties,' Josie said. 'Go
with Leo. It doesn't matter about boys.'

'Leo's going to ask Ian.'

'Oh well.'

Sandy saw that there was no way she could ask
Josie to take Gertie, as Gertie could not possibly

121

fit in here. The idea was a non-starter. Gertie could never climb the lighthouse stairs to bed. Josie, as if telepathic, enquired about Gertie, and Sandy unloaded her moans, which made her feel better.

'She just sits in the chair all day, talking, talking, talking. She doesn't help at all. Yet in her cottage she used to be buzzing about all day. She drives us all nuts.'

'Mum ought to get the social services. If she goes back to her cottage in the summer they could look after her there. After all, Mum used to. I'm sure it'll get sorted out.'

'She's always criticizing. You wouldn't mind if – if—'

'If she was nice? No. I always thought she was a terrible old bag. You and Mum were always the nicest to her.'

Sandy ate three more shortbreads and Josie made coffee. Selina was given two saucepan lids to play with.

Sandy told Josie about losing the thirty pounds, and about Polly losing twenty.

'That's the worst, worse than Gertie. I haven't told Mum and Dad. It must be someone around, someone we know.'

'You ought to tell them!'

'It was my fault, leaving it there. I can't! They'll be so angry.' She couldn't even begin to tell Josie about suspecting first Duncan, then Ian.

She wished she hadn't mentioned it, as Josie, instead of comforting, seemed about to launch an attack on her handling of her affairs. But at the opportune moment the door opened and Glynn came in. He carried a huge basket of wood offcuts for the stove.

'Hey, good timing! Coffee's up.' He shrugged round and bawled out of the open door, 'Jonas, coffee!' He dumped the basket at Sandy's feet. 'Hi, Sandy. How's things? Saw your nag tied up out there. It's the in thing round here, horse transport. We'll have to put up a hitching rail.'

He picked up Selina and flung her in the air. She screamed with delight. The quiet room seemed suddenly to have burst into life with Glynn's arrival. The outdoor sunlight came in with him, along with the smell of fresh wood and damp earth. His fair hair stuck up like a halo round his head. His presence was very positive, and Sandy thought how lucky Josie was to have such a rock of a man to be her partner. Laughing, they looked incredibly handsome together, like an advertisement photo. Selina wriggled in the crook of Glynn's arm and Josie took her, hitching her over her shoulder so that the baby's gold hair glowed against her own blue-black tumble.

Sandy was impressed by seeing everything that home life should be, as compared to what it suddenly wasn't any more at Drakesend. No wonder she got confused. She remembered the endless

tirades from her father, condemning Glynn –
impossible to think that all that heartache had
resolved into this picture of domestic bliss.

While she was being dazzled by this scene,
Jonas Brown slipped hesitantly through the door.
Sandy saw him and felt her face blazing scarlet,
out of control. She wanted to die. She crouched
over Glynn's log-basket, making a pretence of
putting wood on the embers of the fire.

'Sandy, you know Jonas, don't you? Jonas,
Sandy.' Josie made a sketchy introduction. 'You'll
stay and have a coffee, Jonas? Here, sit down.'

She pulled out a chair at the table. Glynn took
Selina back and Josie got out more cups and
saucers. They were her own, covered with red-
and-blue parrots.

'Shortbread?'

She shoved across a plateful.

'Sandy's got to go to a party at the Speerwells',
Glynn. I said you'd take her.'

'No!' Sandy squeaked. 'Don't be daft!'

'What's wrong with me?' Glynn grinned. 'Not
handsome enough?'

'Too old,' said Josie. 'Besides, I'd be jealous.
Hey, you could take her, Jonas! How about that?'

Sandy wanted to die. How *could* Josie be so
crass? Had she really forgotten, already, what it
felt like to be such a quivering bundle of hopes and
confusions, despairs and self-loathing and wild
ambition, that seemed to characterize this state of

adolescent love? Or had she been so confident in her pursuit of men that she had never experienced her insides dying, her brain disintegrating?

'They have great parties, the Speerwells. The food is out of this world. You'd take her, wouldn't you, Jonas?'

What else could he say? Sandy heard him mumble that yes, he wouldn't mind. Have a shortbread? Thanks. How many sugars in your coffee? Just one thanks. Sandy sat by the stove with her head drooping, her heart thumping like a clapped-out diesel engine. She could have killed Josie.

'I must go,' she mumbled.

'You haven't drunk your coffee,' Josie pointed out amiably. 'Here, I made a chocolate cake. I forgot. It needs eating.'

She was a fabulous cook. No-one could depart in the face of such a cake, thick with chocolate icing. Jonas, thin as a reed, ate as if he had never met chocolate cake in his life.

'Who cooks at yours, Jonas?' Josie asked him. 'Your father?'

'We go to the chippy. Or get pies from the shop.'

'No wonder you look half-starved.'

In the ensuing banter Sandy began to recover, slipping up to the table to sit opposite Jonas. She would never get this opportunity again. Catch her going to Speerwell's party after this! She kept stealing quick glances at Jonas. In close-up his gypsy looks were confirmed: his skin brown, his hair black and curling. He had dark brown eyes with long lashes and a quick, secret way of looking as if he, too, were not too sure of his ground. He had a quiet, graceful way of moving that spoke of an outdoor life. He would be useful to Glynn, Sandy could see: skilful with an axe, smart with machinery. He probably did not read much and his writing would be slow and laboured. He was magic with horses. Sandy wanted to know so many things, but could not speak.

Jonas ate three pieces of chocolate cake.

'You'd better not bring him too often, Glynn,' Josie joked.

Jonas flushed up, and Sandy felt herself glowing in sympathy.

'He's worth a chocolate cake. He's a good worker,' Glynn said. He made a date with Jonas to collect some more timber from the top wood. Sandy, in passing, recognized that it was her father's timber that Glynn was taking. Ian had been offered the use of a tractor to do the same job, but had never got round to it, although he was always short of money. Ian was not an outdoor man.

'I must go – tide to catch,' Jonas mumbled.

A tide? Sandy went out with him, saying she had to go back. She thought she could ride as far as the sea-wall with him, unless he went off at his usual gallop. Josie came out with them, the baby on her hip.

'You should come more often,' Josie said to Sandy.

'Yes.' Sandy thought so too. She hadn't realized what a gruelling life the livery yard had been during the last few months. 'I'll have more time in the summer. When it's light.'

She untied George and clambered into the saddle while Jonas whistled Queen Moon and vaulted on to her back. But instead of galloping away, he held back and waited for Sandy.

'She enjoys a bite of grass,' he said.

'Doesn't she go out at all?'

'No. I got nowhere.'

'You could bring her to ours. Our field.'

'Then how do I ride? Walk over?' He laughed. It was about five miles.

'Where did you get her from? She's so lovely.'

'Newmarket. She was too small to race – they threw her out. Lad I know, he told me. He loved her, didn't want her to go to the knacker's. I got her for carcass money. He paid most of it, to save her.'

Sandy digested this. She thought it was only girls who were like that. Soft.

'I might have to go away for a while. If I do, she can come in your field?'

'Yes. Oh yes.'

The two horses walked side by side down towards the sea-wall. It was like a summer's day, the sky cloudless. Sandy felt her heart rising up in her like a balloon, lifting her up. She thought she might float away. At the bottom, he turned left, she turned right. He never said anything about taking her to the party.

Sandy wanted her ride to last for ever. She rode on the bank, slowly, watching the bright sun on the water. The tide was high, lipping at the wall, and the long-billed curlews flew over making their haunting, rippling cries. She could smell the sea and the warming earth and all her troubles dissolved like her breath on the soft air. He spoke to me, she thought.

Just before she got to the track up to Drakesend, two fishing smacks came down the river on the tide, going out to sea. Normally, she never gave the boats a second glance, but this time, taking in everything with her new, seeing eyes, she saw a boy on the foredeck, flaking down a mooring warp. It was Jonas. At the ship's helm was hunched a gypsy-looking man with fierce eyes and a scowl. He was shouting at Jonas, but the words were indistinguishable above the thump of the diesel engine.

Sandy pulled up on top of the wall, watching . . . so that's what he did! He was a fisherman. Everything slotted into place: his funny hours for riding, to fit in with the tides, his air of belonging to another place – a being apart. He worked the smack with his father.

As she watched, he straightened up, finishing his task. He looked up and saw her, and lifted a hand to wave.

Sandy told Leo what had happened, although she hadn't intended to.

'So he's taking you to the party!' Leo was deeply impressed.

'No, of course not! It was Josie's daft remark, but he never made a date or anything. I expect he'd die rather than take me.'

'Who are you going with then?'

'Nobody. You.'

Leo looked gloomy. She had asked Ian, and Ian had said he was going with Julia. 'Blooming cheek. *She* asked him!'

'He's always stuck up for her rather,' Sandy remarked, remembering how Ian had gone on the day she had made her terrible remark. At least Leo had gone off Julia now, which helped.

'It doesn't matter. We can go together.'

'I thought Julia was in love with Tony.'

'Yes, but Tony fancies Polly. Haven't you noticed?'

'She's miles older than him.'

'It's all this schooling together. Every night. I never dreamed he'd get so keen.'

Polly's strong will had prevailed upon Tony Speerwell and his riding had noticeably improved. They rode out together every night looking for cross-country jumps and King of the Fireworks had started to have faith in his rider as Tony learned to keep in tune with him. Tony was athletic and not unintelligent, and the thought of earning his auntie's money kept him wonderfully on his toes. Also, as his confidence grew, he enjoyed it.

'Who wouldn't, with a horse like that?' as Leo remarked.

Leo rode Empress of China more and more. Sandy wanted to make the fourth member of the team and rode the Empress as often as she could, but by the time she had done all the odd jobs round the yard, there wasn't much opportunity. Faithful would jump anything for Julia and had an assured place in the team. Polly was already looking for schedules to find their first competition. Sandy reconciled herself, as always, to being a spectator. She hadn't seen Jonas again, since her visit to Josie. That had all been a dream, too. Sometimes she wondered if that day had really happened. She wanted to ask Josie, but there was never any time to see her. Josie came over to see her mother with the baby, but mostly when Sandy was at school. Sandy went back into her gloom, dreading the party.

'What are you going to wear?' Leo asked her.

'What am I going to wear?' Sandy wept at her mother.

'Parties are supposed to be happy things,' her mother pointed out. 'Josie goes to parties in those red dungarees. I thought it didn't matter these days.'

Sandy wondered about borrowing the dungarees, but Josie was stick-thin. She didn't have a pot like Sandy. Sandy breathed in and stood upright, and found she looked much better. Short skirts were in. Sandy had strong legs like tree-trunks. Standing up and breathing in didn't make them look any better.

Julia had masses of clothes.

'Come to mine and have a look through,' she said.

Sandy had never been to Julia's, so accepted her invitation out of curiosity. Julia's mother had come to terms with her daughter's preferred way of life and now paid Faithful's livery bill, and when Sandy arrived in her kitchen she was friendly in her sergeant-majorish way: 'Sit here. Take those muddy shoes off. Tea or coffee?'

Mrs Marsden had found that driving Nick and Petra hard used up all her energies and fortunately they seemed to enjoy it, so Julia was let off the hook.

'Lucky for me,' Julia remarked. She opened

the wardrobe doors in her bedroom and revealed miles of shelving and hanging space, all apparently packed with pristine clothes. Sandy could get all her clothes in one chest of drawers without even squashing them. She didn't know where to start looking.

'What are you going to wear?'

'This.' Julia pulled out a tiny crimson dress. It was mini and had a plain round neck and short sleeves. Sandy knew that it would look stunning on little waif-like Julia, who had no bulges.

'I want something more – more swamping.'

'Dark,' said Julia. 'Fat people look better in dark colours.'

In her usual stark way she was being helpful. She pulled out some silk shirts in purple and navy and forest-green.

'These look OK loose, with jeans.'

They were miles better than anything Sandy had. They looked expensive and slithered over her arms in a luxurious way.

'Look in the long mirror.' Julia's bedroom had its own bathroom, and a whole wall of mirror. Sandy looked and realized that Julia was right: fat people did look better in dark colours. When she straightened up and held her breath, she looked quite reasonable. She chose the purple shirt. None of Julia's trousers fitted her.

'That'll look fine with jeans,' Julia said.

She wouldn't stand out, but she wouldn't be an

object of scorn. Sandy was satisfied with that.

Julia's room was ablaze with rosettes. There were framed photographs of her show-jumping, and one of her receiving a rosette from Princess Anne. The bedroom had cream carpet all over and a pink flounced bed. Unlike Sandy's, it was as warm as the kitchen below.

'It's funny, what you did,' Sandy said. 'Giving up all this.' She waved her arm towards the rosettes. 'Coming to us.'

Out of the window she could see a stable-yard all painted and perfect, everything in its place and of the best, with no trails of straw or forgotten buckets, no uncoiled hose or thrown-down head-collars. It was a far cry from the tatty yard at Drakesend which, try as she might, Sandy could never get looking any better than 'homely'.

'Oh, it's much nicer at yours,' Julia said as if there could be no argument. 'My ma knows I'd never come back here.'

'Why not?'

'She can't help it. If I came back she'd want me to take Faithful to shows all the time. Faithful'll jump anything now, with me. I could get her right to the top. But she doesn't want to do that, does she? It's stupid. I just like messing about, like we do. Ride how you feel like. I'm really lucky my ma doesn't go on about it all the time – I thought she would. She did for a bit, but she's given up now.'

Sandy realized that even the sergeant-major could see she had met her match in her own daughter. Little, pretty Julia was hard as stone, just like her own mother. She did what she wanted to do.

'It's lucky she's got Nick and Petra to work on. They love it. If she hadn't got them—' Julia shrugged. 'It might be different. They all leave me alone now.'

Sandy had always thought Julia was hard to get to know, but realized now that perhaps her family thought the same. She was unnervingly her own person, not bothering what anyone thought about her. And while everyone about her was striving to make their horses competitive, she went her own way, jumping only what was in her path, not bothered with Polly's rails, coffins and combinations. Polly did not press her, for they all knew that Julia only had to point Faithful at them for the little mare to jump.

For a hopeful, fleeting moment Sandy thought . . . 'You're not keen on being in Polly's team-chase, then?'

'Not really. But they need me, if Tony's got to win his auntie's money.'

No false modesty there. Anyway, George would never get round – what was she dreaming of? In her heart, Sandy knew that Leo would get chosen for the ride on Empress of China. She was a better rider and had more drive

Julia was not the sort to offer words of encouragement or comfort. Sandy felt cast down – about loving Jonas, about being fat and not looking anything much, about growing out of George and not having another pony, about her missing livery money – but Julia did not sense her mood. They talked for a bit about show-jumping, and then Sandy went home with the shirt in a plastic bag.

She tried it on with her best jeans and Gertie said, 'You look pregnant in that thing.'

'Don't be silly, Gertie. Everyone wears loose-fitting clothes today,' Mary Fielding said sharply. 'It's lovely, Sandy.'

'I had a dress once all covered in beads. It hung down just like that. I did the Charleston in it. With Tubby Malone. He asked me to marry him.'

'He married Edith Edmonds – her with the big mole,' Grandpa said.

'Aye, and she were in love with Percy who helped the blacksmith, but Tubby were a good catch, weren't he? I turned him down because 'e 'ad smelly feet. They were terrible. Did you know that? He 'ad a nice home and a good job but I couldn't live with a man with those feet.'

'He could 'ave kept 'is boots on.' Grandpa started his wheezing laugh and then his coughing, and Mary had to fetch him a glass of water. Sandy ran out of the room, wanting to scream. She ran up to her bedroom, which was cold and had only a moth-eaten rug by the bed and no bathroom adjoining, and threw the purple shirt on the bed. She dreaded the party now worse than ever.

Mary Fielding drove them to the party in the car – Sandy and Ian, Julia and Leo. Afterwards, she was going out with Bill to see some friends, and the old couple would have to make their own cocoa and get themselves to bed.

'Gertie won't, bet you,' Ian said. 'You've spoilt her something rotten, Mum. She'll wait till you get back.'

'She'd better not! She's perfectly capable.'

'We all know that, but you—'

'Oh, don't tell me what I've done wrong, *please*! Do you think I don't know?'

Mary changed gear with a jerk, and they all exchanged glances in the back. It was March and the evening was only just going dark. The sky was deep blue and flecked with stars and there was a smell of everything starting, damp and fresh, and the hint of the sea beyond the walls and the marshes. Sandy loved evenings like this, and would sometimes stand down by the ponies' gate just smelling the air. She had reconciled herself to the party being nothing special, only the food, and was facing it with a curious sort of stoicism. She just had to get through it and try and enjoy herself. They had clubbed together, including Polly, and bought Tony a new numnah for King of the Fireworks.

When they got to Brankhead Hall, they piled out at the gate. There was a long gravel drive leading to the house, with a fine avenue of lime trees, and several cars passed them as they walked up. Brankhead Hall was in the stately league, a large early-Victorian, stucco-fronted pile with a fine porch. The gravel drive swept round majestically, edged by elegant lawns, and the house was framed by huge old trees. The cars were disappearing round the side to some hidden parking, decanting their passengers at the brightly lit door. The passengers seemed older and smarter than the party from Drakesend, who hesitated before the porch. Through the open door they could see waitresses standing with trays of drinks.

'Cor,' said Ian softly.

In a lull they moved forward. As they did so, a figure detached itself from the shadows beside the porch and came to meet them. It was Jonas.

'Hi, Sandy,' he said.

Sandy nearly keeled over on the spot.

'Jonas!'

Apart from not being on Queen Moon he looked just the same as he always did, in jeans and a dark sweater with a hole in the elbow. Not for him long evenings agonizing over what to wear.

'I – I thought—' Sandy didn't know what she thought.

They went in and a man took their scruffy anoraks and the waitresses offered up the trays of drinks. Sandy took something she thought was orange juice, and found out very soon that it wasn't. Jonas didn't take one at all. The others all took champagne. Sandy thought, 'Mum's not going to like this.' She felt intoxicated and she hadn't taken a sip yet.

Tony was standing a little further in, looking like an advert for aftershave – so glossy and beautiful. They had improved him – both Sandy and Leo had the same thought: he was much nicer since he had started coming to Drakesend, not so prone to giving orders. Nobody took any notice of him at Drakesend, and he had discovered that everybody did nearly everything better than he did, which had been a salutary surprise. They could see, from his mother, that he hadn't had a good start in life and, having been so struck by the beauty of Brankhead Hall, Sandy remembered that father Speerwell had bought it with the intention of knocking it all down and building flats.

Tony's party manners were splendid as, after he had greeted them, he took Leo away to dance, aware that she was the unaccompanied one. Ian and Jonas went to look for food, but it was too early: a bevy of butlers and waitresses shooed them away from the groaning tables, so they went and sat on the stairs. These rose elegantly out of the middle of the large hall, and all the party rooms opened off the hall so they got a good view of what was going on. Ian and Jonas started to talk about diesel engines, so Sandy and Julia sat in silence on the steps below them. Julia looked fabulous in her short red dress with her white unspotted complexion and her hairstyle, which looked as if she had been out in the rain, and a boy in their sixth form came up and asked her to dance. She departed, and Leo came back and sat with Sandy.

'So he's come!' she hissed. 'Lucky beggar.'

'It's only because Josie made him.'

'He must have wanted to.'

Leo had put make-up on and looked rather peculiar, sort of browner than usual, as if she had been skiing. Her eyes looked very large. Sandy looked to see if her ears had gone pointed; she looked like an elf. She was taller than Julia but just as wraithlike and wore black shorts and a gold sloppy top. Sandy felt old-fashioned. Ian and Jonas were talking about filters.

'Let's dance,' Leo said, after about half an hour.

They went down the stairs and into the room where the music was, where they jigged about in a corner watching all the others. There were not many people they knew. Polly had arrived, wearing an amazing silver tube with enormous feathers round the top, and was dancing with Tony. She must have brought Henry, her dressage protégé – who was getting rather neglected since the team-chase had become serious – as he suddenly

140

appeared before the two girls and started jigging about in company.

'Great place this.'

Henry, it was suddenly revealed, was a terrific dancer. Afterwards, Sandy supposed that dressage was all about rhythm and timing and impulsion, and Henry, divorced from his mount Dodo, seemed to be able to do it much better on his own two legs. The human equivalent of flying changes and pirouettes convulsed his lean frame, along with much dynamic body-toting which even Sandy found quite inspiring. With two partners he commanded his corner of the room. Soon Julia joined them with her sixth-form admirer, Mark, and the five of them continued with wild abandon until they noticed that everyone else was drifting away to eat.

'Wow, Henry, never knew you had it in you!'

The girls were exhausted. Whatever it was that she had drunk, along with the action, made Sandy feel that the room was turning circles. She, who didn't think she could dance, had danced like a dervish. Wonders would never cease. She even began to think she might be enjoying herself. Ian and Jonas had disappeared.

They went into the food place. Sandy could feel the sweat trickling down her face. Leo, she noticed, was looking streaky, but Julia looked as cool as ever. The dancing had given them an appetite. The food was laid out on long tables with large plates at the ready: not just bites, but great bowlfuls of coronation chicken, plates of ham and beef and jacket potatoes and salads of every variety – beans, rice, lettuce, tomato, carrot, beetroot – and bread rolls by the mountain. For afters there were platefuls of pavlovas and meringues and tarts and profiteroles and trifle and large cheeseboards and baskets of biscuits. The waitresses kept filling up glasses. Sandy and Leo piled their plates high. It was all too good to miss.

'Where've Ian and Jonas got to?'

They found them sitting under banks of camellias in the conservatory – a quiet corner which they had to themselves. Their plates were now nearly empty, but had been piled ingeniously high and wide with helpings of everything, except lettuce. Julia went off with Mark.

Sandy had some more 'orange juice' and began to feel very optimistic about life. Why had she thought she didn't like parties? They ate so much they could hardly move. This was no way to get slim, she remembered thinking hazily. She could stare at Jonas now without feeling embarrassed, realizing that he was – although one wouldn't know it – her partner at this fabulous dance. Great red camellias blossomed above his gorgeous dark head, as if he was wearing them in his gypsy hair. When the music started again she had the nerve to say to him, 'Come and dance.'

'And you, Ian,' Leo said firmly.

They got reluctantly to their feet. They couldn't dance like Henry, but they jigged about obediently. Sometimes, as the evening progressed, the music was slow and smoochy, and Sandy saw that all the old people (and there were quite a lot of them) danced in each other's arms and put their cheeks together. It looked really dreamy and she had a great longing to dance like that with Jonas – how fabulous it would feel to have his body so close to hers, and his curls brushing her face (except he was a fair bit taller than she was). These old fogeys knew a thing or two. She recalled Gertie and her tale of dancing the Charleston – perhaps she and Grandpa had danced here in their day? Grandpa had worked for the squire of Brankhead Hall for several years. In their twirling she noticed Polly float by in Tony's arms. Her eyes were shut and he held her very close and had a great mouthful of feathers to contend with. Julia was swaying chest to chest with Mark, the sixth-former, hardly moving at all, and Mark had his arms round her in a thoroughly old-fashioned way. Oh, Jonas, Sandy thought, love me like that. But she knew life wasn't like that for her.

'Ma said she'd come at twelve,' Ian remarked. It was five to. 'We'd better go and look for her.'

Was it over already? Sandy looked at Jonas.

'Shall I take you home?' he asked her suddenly. He must have borrowed his father's car.

'Oh, yes!'

'There's plenty of room in our car,' Ian said.

'Oh, don't be stupid, Ian,' Leo said sharply. She turned away. 'I'll tell Julia.'

She was jealous, Sandy thought. So would I be. She drifted away on her cloud to get her coat. Jonas waited for her at the front door. They went out together.

'Not bad, was it?' he said.

'Oh, no, it was wonderful!'

He led the way past the shrubberies to the field behind the house where all the cars were parked. The river glittered below. There was a nearly full moon and only the softest of breezes. Jonas walked with his hands in his pockets, smooth and purposeful. He went past all the cars and climbed the wooden fencing into the field below.

'I left her here – it's lovely grass,' he said, and whistled. Out of the moonlight came his beautiful mare, her ears pricked up, the halter tied up round her neck. She stood waiting for him, like a silver ghost.

Sandy could not believe it. Jonas seemed to take it completely for granted.

'She'll have enjoyed it as much as we did,' he said, grinning. 'The gate's not locked. Just the ticket.' He held out a hand. 'I'll give you a leg-up.'

She put out her foot and he hoicked her up on Queen Moon's back. Sandy felt the mare's flanks warm under her jeans. She was narrow after George and her mane lifted in the breeze. Jonas walked over and opened the gate, and Sandy rode the mare through. He shut it behind them, then vaulted up behind Sandy, a hand for a moment on her thigh. Their bodies fitted together, just like the old fogeys dancing. Only it was better, a thousand times better. Sandy didn't know whether to laugh or cry. It was better than any of her dreams, something beyond dreams, to ride with Jonas on Queen Moon.

Queen Moon walked quickly and when she got to the sea-wall she went to turn left, for home, but Jonas turned her with his legs in the other direction. She went obediently, without hesitation. Jonas had one arm round Sandy, holding the rope rein, and she could feel the other on his thigh, touching hers. They moved in unison to the mare's movement. Jonas seemed content to walk.

The tide was high and the water glittered in the moonlight. Wading birds trilled along the water-line, their calls returned like echoes from far away across the marshes.

'I was going to ask you,' Jonas said, in her ear. 'If – if I go away, will you look after my mare?'

'Yes, of course.'

'I might not be able to pay you.'

'It doesn't matter.'

'Just in the field, she won't need a stable.'

145

'I'll look after her. Why are you going away?'

'I can't live with my father any more. I want a job, on my own.'

'Where?'

'I want to get on a trawler. Or, if not, try for an oil-rig.'

She wouldn't see him any more. Ah well. She knew.

Perhaps that was why he had taken her to the dance, to ask her this.

'Do you want to gallop?' He bent his head and whispered in her ear. But she wanted it to last for ever.

'Yes,' she said, because he wanted her to say yes.

She hardly felt the transition, so smooth the mare's take-off, so easy her movement. She went like a ghost horse, as if the hard ground was a cloud under her hooves, and Jonas bent close to Sandy and put both arms round her. Perhaps he didn't want her to fall off. Perhaps he loved her. Sandy loved him with all her being. She kept thinking to herself: remember this, take in every detail. Nothing so wonderful will ever happen to you again. The moon came out, larger than life, and their shadow chased them below the wall, their bodies clinging as one. I shall never forget this, Sandy thought, not till the day I die. Like Gertie and the Charleston. When I am really old like Gertie I shall remember Jonas.

She slipped down at the driveway to Drakes-end. Jonas turned the mare to go back, and waved his hand.

'Goodbye,' he said.

And rode away.

The next morning, when Sandy went into the tackroom, she found four saddles missing: Polly's, Tony's, Arthur's and Henry's. At first, she could not believe the evidence of her eyes. She thought their owners had all gone for a ride. But the horses were still in their looseboxes. It was only eight o'clock and no-one had come yet.

She ran back up to the house and told her parents. They were stunned.

'They're worth about three hundred each! Polly's is worth more – and Henry's.' Henry's was a dressage saddle, his pride and joy. It was worth more than his horse.

'At least we're insured,' Bill said.

'That's not the point,' his wife said bitterly. *Who is doing it?*

'We were all out. Someone knew!'

At least, Sandy thought, it wasn't Tony or Polly or Ian or Leo or Julia or Henry – or Jonas. Then she realized the saddles could have been taken after the party. Any time up until she had gone out there at eight o'clock that morning.

'The police must know this time,' Mary said.

'But is it an inside job?' Bill wondered. 'It could be tricky, if it turns out that way.'

'Why, who do you suspect? Grandpa?'

Sandy saw that her mother was almost in tears. Did she suspect someone?

'We could catch them!' Sandy said. 'I could sleep in the loft over the tackroom. Every night! And then I'd see.'

'It might come to that,' said her father. 'Leave a trap – something valuable.'

'No. You must tell the police,' Mary said. 'They'll have to know, because of the insurance claims. Was the door locked?'

'Yes, I always lock it.'

'Was the lock broken? How did he get in?'

'Nothing was out of place.' Sandy thought back over it. She had unlocked the door as she always did and it was undisturbed. The windows were shut and locked. They kept another key hidden under the water-butt by the feed-shed. Everyone in the yard knew about the spare key, in case they wanted their tack when Sandy had locked up. It happened quite often.

'Whoever did it knows about the spare key.'

'Then it *is* an inside job.'

Sandy saw her parents looked sort of saggy, as if they had been punched. She felt rather sick. She kept thinking of Duncan. He came at six o'clock.

149

How could he steal four saddles, on a bicycle? You'd need a car.

'We'll have a talk, when Polly and the others come,' Bill decided. 'It's their property, after all, not ours. Try not to let anyone in the tackroom, Sandy – there might be fingerprints, if we get the police in.'

The others were rather late, as might be expected. Sandy felt that her dream-world, so close, had disintegrated into the worst sort of nightmare. A friend had done this, it seemed. What sort of friends did they have? When Tony arrived he was wearing a beautiful new leather jacket, his birthday present from his parents. Sandy could not stop herself thinking, Don't take it off, Tony, whatever you do.

He said breezily, 'We'll have to buy new ones! Nothing's safe these days.'

Polly, predictably, went white.

'I'll never get another saddle like that one! It cost me an arm and a leg. The insurance never pay you in full – and they're far more expensive now. Whatever shall I do?'

Bill Fielding rang the police. 'Whoever it was, only took the good ones.' The pony saddles, and Stick and Ball's antediluvian old plates, were still on their racks.

Nobody could ride.

'And I've found a team-chase for us, a novice class, the very thing – only a month from now!' Polly despaired. 'We can't stop work at this stage.'

'We can get some second-hand saddles to tide us over,' Tony said. 'My parents'll pay for them – we can pay them back when we get the insurance money.'

Polly and Henry perked up slightly at this. But they loved their own saddles. 'With luck the police will get them back.'

But there was very little to go on. The police came down and examined everything, but found no fingerprints, no footmarks, no sign of force. The outside key was in its appointed place; nothing was out of place.

'He must have had a car.' But it was impossible to find any incriminating tracks.

Polly and Tony arranged to have an outing to buy new saddles and in a few days they were back to normal. But Sandy could take no joy in the stables any more. It was all right for Tony and Polly – they were only onlookers, although their property was concerned. But they weren't responsible for the place, as Sandy was. She begged to be allowed to sleep in the loft over the tackroom.

'It's warm enough, and no-one will know I'm there. I'll find out, if anyone comes. It's the only way!'

'I don't like the idea,' said her mother. 'It could be dangerous.'

'It's a good idea,' said Gertie. 'Get that rotter who pinched my money.'

Talking about it gave Mary Fielding her opening to suggest that Gertie might feel like moving back to her cottage.

'I'll go back when the weather improves,' Gertie said. But nobody could tell whether she meant it.

'Oh, please, Mum, let me sleep over there,' Sandy begged. 'Leo could come too. We could do it together. And he wouldn't know we were there. We'd be perfectly safe.'

To her surprise, her father thought it was a good idea.

'We could lay a bait. Leave something in the tackroom that might tempt him.' Everyone took their saddles home with them since the break-in.

'Like what?' Ian asked scornfully. 'Sandy?'

'Ha ha,' said Sandy.

They all tried to think of something valuable that would look as if it belonged, and not like a trap.

'A really good bike is worth a bit these days. How about Ian's mountain bike?' Sandy suggested. 'It would be a perfectly reasonable place to keep it.'

Her parents thought it a good idea. Ian didn't. He was overruled.

'The whole point is, if it goes this time, Sandy will see who takes it.'

'Huh. She'll be snoring like a trooper.'

152

'I will not!'

Leo's parents didn't like the idea, but Leo over-ruled them. Mary Fielding promised to give her breakfast and get her off to school. Leo thought the plan a great lark. The two girls spent a private evening carving lookout holes in the floor of the loft (and the ceiling of the tackroom) and in all the side walls so that they had a good view in every direction, and – when no-one was about – they took two campbeds up there with their bedding. Ian's bike took up residence in the tackroom. Everyone fell over it and complained. Tony bought King of the Fireworks a very ex-pensive Melton rug for going to team-chases and this was displayed prominently, looking very de-sirable. 'Cost me a few quid,' he boasted. The trap was sprung.

The first night they were to sleep there, Sandy and Leo went to bed early. It was eight o'clock and just going dark. Sandy put the light on.

'He won't come till everyone's asleep.'

'You're not expecting him tonight, are you? That would be too easy. It'll probably take weeks, long after we've got fed up with sleeping up here. Or he might never come.'

But there was something both exciting and cosy about their new situation. It was fun to be sleeping together, to be on their own without anyone else. They wriggled down into their sleep-ing bags. The evening breezes whistled through the old loft and starlings cluttered and chattered in the eaves.

'I hope there's no rats,' Leonie said.

'No. The cats keep them away.'

'Tony's party was great. Pity it finished with the saddles being nicked.'

'At least it can't have been Jonas.'

'You didn't think he'd come, did you?'

'No. I was sure he wouldn't. But he only came because Josie told him to. I could have died.'

'He wouldn't have come if he hadn't wanted to, daftie. He enjoyed it. He's quite civilized really.'

'The ride home was—' Sandy had already tried to describe it to Leo – tried and failed. She thought she would never forget that evening till her dying day. She hadn't seen Jonas since. It was no good pretending it had been the start of a great love affair.

They gossiped, knowing it was going to be hard to get to sleep the first night. It was strange, when they stopped talking: the shuffling and munching and sighing of the horses drifted up from the yard, and the muttering and chuckling of the Brent geese on the marshes carried so clearly on the still night air that they could have been in the yard too.

'I suppose we ought to put the light out.'

Sandy lay there thinking about it, and in that instant they both heard quite clearly the sound of the key turning in the tackroom padlock below.

Sandy heard Leo give a sort of gulp. They looked at each other. Sandy felt the hairs rising up on the back of her neck. She lay petrified, not daring to move. Footsteps sounded on the floor below.

Sandy knew she should apply her eye to the hole in the floor, but she was too frightened to make a move. The two campbeds creaked alarmingly every time they moved. Whoever it was must know they were there, because of the light – who was going to discover whom?

The footsteps paused. There was an agonizing silence. Then the footsteps approached the ladder and the two girls heard someone coming up.

Afterwards, comparing notes, they both agreed they were so frightened they nearly passed out. They heard the groping hand looking for the trapdoor edge, then the trapdoor started to lift. Sandy heard Leo give a sort of squeak.

The trapdoor rose up and a head followed it.

'Good heavens!'

It was Duncan.

'I thought you'd left the light on. I didn't know you were still here.'

No-one knew who was the most surprised. Duncan now looked thoroughly embarrassed.

'I was just on my way home. Sorry if I frightened you.'

'We're doing a burglar watch.'

'Yeah, I can guess. I used the spare key. It's very easy for this burglar.'

'We're setting a trap. We want to see who it is.'

'You'll be sorry.'

Sandy, propped up on one elbow, said quickly, 'What do you mean?'

Duncan, in the poor light, looked even more embarrassed. 'I'll be getting along. I'm sorry if I spoilt it.'

'No,' said Leo. 'You didn't. It's good practice. I didn't know how terrified I'd feel. We were really stupid to leave the light on. We didn't think he'd come till much later.'

'You're probably right.'

'Do you know who it is?' Sandy asked.

There was a long silence. Duncan, framed in the trapdoor, looked very solid and dependable, Sandy thought – how could she ever have suspected him? He never skimped on his work, sitting up with sick cows, coming now to put the light off when he could easily have ignored it. She still had his penknife in her anorak pocket.

'Do you know?' she repeated.

Duncan shrugged. He had shoulders like a rugger player, and a wide, mild face, not easily excited. He always needed a haircut and quite often a shave.

'Sometimes it's best not to know things.'

'What does that mean?' Leo asked sharply.

'It hurts.'

'Who is it?'

156

'I don't know,' he said.

They thought he was lying. His face was expressionless.

'I'd best get along. I'll lock the padlock and put the key back. I'm sorry if I scared you.'

When he had gone, they put the light out and lay there going over his remarks. They were both very disturbed. Sandy was agonized.

Leo said, 'Perhaps it was a cover for himself, to appear to be so helpful and cast the blame away from himself.'

'Oh, no. Not Duncan.' Sandy hadn't told even Leo about the penknife. 'I wish that hadn't happened.'

'I was so terrified. If the burglar does come, we'll be useless. We'll just die of fright.'

'Everything squeaks so up here. We can't even move to look through the holes. I suppose if he comes by car, we could look out before he gets in.'

It wasn't a good start. Sandy told her mother – not her father – what Duncan had said, about being sorry if they knew who it was. Mary Fielding did not reply, but her saggy look came back and she looked about sixty.

'Do you know?' Sandy shouted out, the agony feeling coming back.

Her mother shouted back at her, 'Nobody *knows*! You just think, without any proof. That's what's so horrible about it!'

'Who do you *think* then?'

'Do you think I would tell you, you stupid girl?'

Her mother was so upset that Sandy was scared. All her clever plans suddenly seemed as useless as thistledown drifting on the breeze.

Polly entered their team in the competition under the name 'Drakesend Dodderers'. It was apparently the fashion to use facetious names. It suggested, in true British style, that you did not expect to win. Tony wanted Drakesend Devils, and Ian suggested Drakesend Dumbos. Polly thought she had chosen a happy medium.

'Tony on King of the Fireworks, me on Charlie's Flying, Julia on Faithful, and Leo on Empress of China.'

Sandy accepted the blow as it fell. Although Polly hadn't mentioned it before, Sandy had known Leo would get the ride on Arthur's horse. Polly gave her an anxious glance and Sandy returned a brave smile. Inside, she felt hurt and demolished. 'It's my yard,' she thought indignantly to herself. 'If it wasn't for me, no-one would be here at all. There wouldn't be a team.' Then she thought that that ought to be a comfort, ought to make her feel good and important. It didn't.

Nothing made her feel good any more. Jonas seemed to have disappeared. Mary Fielding was a nervous wreck and always in a bad temper. She had cleaned up Gertie's cottage for Gertie to return to as soon as the weather settled into summer, and now Grandpa said Gertie mustn't leave: Drakesend was his house, and he would say who lived there. As this was true, the argument was very delicate. Josie came round with the baby, and Sandy came in on the tail-end of an argument between Josie and her mother and was in time to see Josie depart in tears. She could not believe her eyes.

'Don't you say a word!' her mother hissed at her. 'I've had it up to here. I don't want to hear your opinion, or anyone else's!'

Sandy, hurt, retired to her bedroom in the loft. It seemed a friendly place all of a sudden. They had made it more cosy now, with books and shelves and a carpet, and they both slept soundly there, almost having forgotten about the burglar. The team-chase was taking precedence in their thoughts, even Sandy's, although she wasn't riding.

'I wish Polly had chosen you,' Leo said gloomily. 'I'm frightened to death. You know what a hold the Empress can take once she's tizzed up.'

'You can still ride better than Tony though. And he's not frightened.'

'Well, he's still as conceited as they come, isn't

he? He doesn't swank about like he used to, but he still has a pretty high opinion of himself.'

'You could call it confidence.'

'You could.' Leo was doubtful.

'He's the one most likely to fall off.'

'But he's the one who's got to get round.'

'Only three have to get round. It's the first three home.'

'I know. But for his auntie's money, he's got to finish.'

'Whatever was in his auntie's mind, he's much nicer since he started coming here. It's worked, hasn't it? Do you remember the night he first came, in the lorry? How bossy he was?'

'Yes. He was revolting.' Leo considered for a moment and said, 'Julia's nicer, too. It must be your influence, Sandy.'

Was Leo being nice, to make up? Sandy wasn't sure.

Polly hadn't asked Julia if she wanted to be in the team: she just took it for granted.

'Do we, Faithful?' Julia asked her. She was sitting in the straw in the corner of the box, watching Faithful feed. Faithful's box was her home-from-home, like the loft for Sandy and Leo. She spent a lot of time in there with Faithful, not just mucking out or grooming, but sitting. Nobody commented on it, taking it for granted. Everybody, if questioned, would have said Julia

161

was a bit odd, a loner, but nobody disliked her. If Julia had been asked what she was doing, sitting in Faithful's box, she would have found it hard to answer. Most of the time she was thinking how nice it was, not being at a show, not loading up or unloading or trying not to forget the bandages, the schedule, the spare girth, the water bucket, the plaiting things. All her life until now she had been chivvied unmercifully. At Drakesend, nobody asked anything of her. Until now.

Faithful was an unusually affectionate pony. Whether she was grateful for Julia after her treatment by her former owners, or whether it was just in her nature to show affection, Julia did not know. But Julia remembered being struck, the first time she had seen her, by the look of misery quite transparent in her demeanour. It was unusual for a horse to show these human emotions quite so clearly: they could look dejected or lively, in general, but rarely 'spoke' of their condition quite so patently as Faithful did. Even in the middle of her feed, Faithful would take time off to give Julia a loving shove. Julia couldn't imagine Big Gun from Minnesota lifting his greedy nose for one instant under the circumstances. This unstinting love gave Julia the best feeling in her life. She felt she had an anchor at Drakesend – her faithful (how well-named!) mare who would never deviate in her loving trust.

'I don't think we want to do team-chasing, do we?' Julia said. 'You might get hurt. The only thing is – they will need us.'

Faithful was only an inch over fourteen hands, and would be markedly smaller than her companions in the team, which meant she would be going flat out to keep up. She was very fit; it wouldn't damage her, but the sport was much rougher than show-jumping and injury came easily. Julia thought she would tell Polly to try and find somebody else – not this first time, because it was too late to change things, but later, when Tony had got going. The competition bug still eluded Julia. She had no desire to win rosettes.

'She's a funny girl,' they all said.

But weren't they all?

When it happened, Sandy and Leo were totally unprepared. It was a Friday night and in the morning they were all going over to have a look at the team-chase course. The competition was the following weekend. According to Polly, it was 'a doddle'.

'But none of us have jumped together over more than a couple of ditches down on the marshes, or over those two fences Tony built up in the wood,' Leo moaned. 'Then we stop. What will it be like over a mile and a half and sixteen fences? They'll get so excited – and pull—'

Sandy was feeling more relieved day by day that it was going to be Leo riding and not herself. Or so she told herself. But sometimes, underneath her encouraging remarks to Leo, there was a big blank of disappointment. She was still the fat dogsbody whom no-one considered for any of the plums of this life: the one who would muck out when the others had gone for a ride, who fetched the furthest horse from the grazing, who mended the torn New Zealand rug when it was unwearable – even when it wasn't her horse's. They all knew she would.

Jonas had disappeared from the planet. Being deeply in love with a disappeared person made life no easier.

She lay in her campbed listening to Leo getting herself in a state, and wondered where she had gone wrong. Leo liked excitement in her life; she enjoyed frightening herself in bed at night. Sandy hadn't the heart to discourage her. She could have said, 'The Empress is very old. She'll probably drop dead after the second fence.' But she didn't. She put the light out and pretended to go to sleep. Leo went on talking to herself for some time, then fell asleep too.

What time it was when they woke up, they had no idea. It was pitch dark. They woke up simultaneously, disturbed by the unfamiliar sound. It was a car at the end of the drive.

'Oh, lawks!' Leo whispered.

They both lay staring at the ceiling. Sandy willed the noise not to have happened. All was now silence.

'Did you hear it?' Leo squawked.

'Yes. Of course.'

He wouldn't come right up, of course, or he would be heard from the farmhouse. He would stop down there, turning the car round to make a getaway towards the village.

Had it been their imagination?

They lay without talking for what seemed like an hour.

'Are we imagining things?' Leo whispered.

'No. Shut up.'

There was no moon, no stars. It was hard to make out even the rafters above.

Faintly, a soft clunk came from the yard. King of the Fireworks whickered. He had seen someone, Sandy knew. It was a quite friendly, curious, surprised whicker. People didn't come to feed them in the middle of the night, but he was optimistic.

Then, from below, they heard the familiar click of the key turning in the lock and the soft squeak of the tackroom door opening.

Neither of the girls had realized how frightened they would be when this eagerly awaited incident happened. Sandy could hear her heart thumping so loudly she thought it must echo through the whole building. She felt insufferably breathless. Leo lay like a dead body beside her, rigid. They had neither of them worked out what they were going to do. Look through the hole in the floor . . . it seemed completely mad now, the dark so all-embracing, the floor squeaky, and the flesh so utterly unwilling. Sandy bit her lip till she could taste blood. She remembered vividly Duncan's head appearing in the trapdoor. Even more vividly she remembered their exchange of words: 'We're setting a trap. We want to see who it is,' and his reply: 'You'll be sorry.' He had covered it up later, but that was what he said. Why?

Was it Ian? He had several friends with cars. Duncan himself, being clever? Sandy couldn't bear it.

She sat up in bed and reached for the light switch. She jumped out and screamed, 'Go away! Go away!'

There was a crash from below and the sound of feet, running.

Leo sat up and screamed, 'You idiot! You idiot!'

Sandy burst into tears.

Leo got up and flung open the trap, switching on her torch. The door below was open and Ian's bike lay half in and half out, its back wheel spinning. The sound of running footsteps floated, echoing for a moment, from under the archway. Leo turned furiously and shone her torch out into the lane.

She screamed, 'We saw you! We saw you! We know who it is!'

'You didn't!' Sandy shouted.

'No, of course not – thanks to you, you idiot, you fool, you nutcase! Why? After all the time we've put in? Are you mad?'

Leo was livid with rage. Her eyes glittered in the torchlight. 'He's gone. I never saw him. How could I?'

They heard the car engine starting up and its rapid retreat in the direction of the village.

Sandy sat up, hugging her knees. Ian wouldn't steal his own bike, surely? Oh, she was glad! She didn't care a toss for Leo's fury. It wasn't anyone they knew. It couldn't be.

'I didn't want to know.'

Leo flumped down on her bed. She was trembling.

'You're so stupid!' But her voice lacked conviction now. 'Why do you say that? Why are you so frightened of who it might be?'

'Of course I am! Of course I am!'

It was all right for Leo – she wasn't involved. It wasn't her farm, her family all falling apart, her mother acting so strangely, her brother so incalculable. Leo didn't know about Duncan's penknife. Sandy felt herself so mixed-up, so weary of this horrible thing hanging over them.

Leo said softly, 'However bad it is, it would be better out in the open. Better solved. Quicker, then, to get right again.'

She was right of course. Sandy started to cry.

'It must be someone in the know,' Leo went on inexorably, 'because he knows about the key, and that there's something here worth stealing.'

'What shall we do?'

She couldn't bear to tell her parents, to upset them all over again. It had been bad enough last time. If she shut her eyes, would it go away? Would the burglar give up, being so frightened?

Leo said, 'It's up to you.'

If she thought she had troubles before this happened, Sandy realized, she had been living in cloud-cuckoo land. Now she had real problems. They both lay on their beds with the light on, trying to get over the shock.

In the end they went downstairs and put the bike back in its place, replaced the key in its hiding-place, shut the door and went back to bed.

'I'll tell them in the morning,' Sandy said.

It would all seem better in the light of day.

In the morning they overslept after their eventful night and when they went in for breakfast there was no-one there. Mary Fielding had gone shopping and Bill was out in the fields. Gertie was still in bed and Grandpa had gone for his tobacco. Ian was still asleep. They made their own breakfast and went back to the stables.

'Don't say anything to the others,' Sandy said. 'They mustn't know before my parents.'

'No.'

Polly and Tony arrived in their respective cars; Julia had gone for a ride early. As soon as she came back, Polly decided, they would all drive over to Aspen Farm to view the team-chase course.

It was a lovely spring day and Tony and Polly were in great spirits. Leo and Sandy could not help but be subdued after their night's adventure, but it went unnoticed. Polly thought Leo was getting cold feet and made encouraging remarks about Empress of China's reliability – no-one had ever mentioned it before, mainly because it wasn't really apparent, but the chatter was welcome and Leo made clever, hopeful replies. Julia returned and put Faithful out in the field, and they all piled into Polly's gruesome car. Tony wanted to drive his own, but they wouldn't let him.

'You're in a team now, mate, and we all have to do everything together,' Polly stated. 'Nothing is for self, all is for the team.'

'I just want to get there,' Tony said mildly.

'Trust me.'

Aspen Farm was some ten miles away, rather off the beaten track and so not a high-powered venue, more a fun course. This was why Polly had chosen it. The land was open and rolling, with clumps of woodland just coming into leaf, and narrow ditches gurgling with spring rainwater. They parked their car in the farmyard and, having asked permission, set out to survey their task. It was too soon for the course to be flagged, but Polly had ridden it before and knew the way.

Sandy was glad now she was out of it. She had enough to worry about without the added terrors of picturing herself out here on an uncontrollable Empress of China.

'All this galloping grass!' Leo wailed. 'She'll cart me for sure.'

'Look,' said Polly severely, 'we're all likely to get carted, save Julia. Charlie's not done this in company before, and we none of us know what King of the Fireworks is like once he gets steam up. So it's no good you looking for sympathy. The thing to remember is: we want to get round. We're not trying to win. There's nothing in the rules to say we've got to gallop flat out. We can trot if necessary. We must all try to keep under control, we must all help each other.'

She then spoilt this sensible harangue by saying, 'It's a super place if you do get out of control – miles and miles of grass. You've only got to go round in circles till the horse gets tired – no problems at all.'

Leo then thought she would probably drop off with exhaustion before they finished: it seemed miles. They set off from the start across a field towards a not-too-awful ditch with a telegraph pole lodged over the top . Over the first and it was right-handed across more grass towards a copse. In front of the copse was a stream made into a coffin jump – a bar in front of it and a bar on the far side, with room inside for the horse to take the stream as a separate jump. Once into the wood the course went down a peaty ride with jumps built at intervals – mostly stacks of fallen timber or fallen trees.

'Slowly through here,' Polly said. 'Just a trot really. It's no place to run amok.'

The jump out was large, up a bank and over.

'But horses are always keen to get out of a wood,' Polly said. 'No problem.'

The problem followed at the next jump where they had to turn and jump into the wood again, which Polly said they wouldn't like.

'Perhaps you should take the lead here, Julia,' Polly said. 'Faithful is probably the most obedient.'

The second loop through the wood was short, with another jump out over a clipped hedge, quite easy, then a long gallop up a grass field like a prairie.

'This will be the problem, keeping in control up here, after all that jumping in the wood. Whatever you do, keep a hold over this jump – don't let them get away with you on landing, when they see this wonderful sea of grass.'

At the top of the field was the catch: the pen, with a slip-rail into it and a jump out, where all the members of the team had to stay inside the pen together before they started to jump out. The fastest had to wait for the slowest, or for the rider who had fallen off and was running up the field on its own legs.

By now even Tony was looking worried. Julia was the only one apparently unaffected by the task ahead.

'I think you might be the key member,' Polly said to her quietly. 'The one who holds us all together.'

Sandy knew that Polly wasn't completely confident of being in full charge herself. Sandy was the only one who had been to hunter trials with Polly and seen how hard her horse was to hold even when going round on his own. Going round with his mates was going to be a great lark.

After the pen there were several jumps across natural hedges and ditches, none too awful, and then a gruelling uphill finish which came back to the same place as the start. By the time they got back to this spot, Sandy was the only really cheerful member of the group. Instead of being jealous of Leo, she was radiantly happy that none of this was going to happen to her. Leo was white as a sheet, Tony unusually quiet, and Polly thoughtful. Julia was her usual enigmatic self.

Polly said, 'The jumps are easy. It's just a matter of being sensible.'

'Not falling off,' said Tony.

'Not bolting,' said Leo.

'Not winning,' said Julia.

'Why not winning?' said Tony.

'Because if you win you're out of the Novice and then you have to ride the Open course.'

'I don't think there's much danger there,' Polly said.

They drove home in a rather quiet mood. Polly said they would walk the course properly, working out tactics, later in the week, and Tony promised he would see about borrowing a horsebox big enough to load all the horses – he had rich friends. Polly would have to make two journeys if she used her decrepit trailer and borrowed a Land Rover.

When they got home they all, except Sandy, went out for a practice ride. Sandy knew she had to go and tell her parents about the visitor in the night, and her miseries came back. Her father was out, but her mother was getting the lunch. Gertie and Grandpa sat in their chairs by the fire. Gertie was knitting a dishcloth (Mary now had seven), and Grandpa was trying to find his pools coupon.

'Mum.' Sandy hovered over the table, her back to the old folk. Her mother was mashing potatoes to put on the shepherd's pie. 'Last night—'

Her mother's gaze switched from her mashing and needled Sandy.

'Somebody came.'

'Don't tell me!' Her mother almost screamed.

'We didn't see! He ran away, because I put the light on and frightened him away. We never saw who it was!'

'Oh, thank God for that!'

Sandy was horrified. It was all right for her, Sandy, to flunk out, but that her mother wanted to . . .

'Mum, why—?'

'Don't tell anyone,' her mother said. 'I can sort it out. Does Leo know? Did she see?'

'Yes, she was awake. But I spoilt it. Neither of us saw who it was.'

'Don't tell your father. Not anybody. Don't let Leo say anything.'

'No, she won't.' But why, she wanted to add? But her mother was tight-lipped, mashing like a dervish.

'Just forget it, Sandy. It's not your worry. It won't happen again.'

'But—'

'Don't talk about it!'

Mary Fielding spread the potato over the pie and put it in the oven. Then she went out.

Sandy felt turned upside down. She had thought her mother would call the police and she would get into trouble for not seeing the vigil through. All that trouble they had gone to, and then to panic at the last moment . . . she had no great opinion of herself. She went to the hearth and sat down in front of the fire, her favourite place, before Gertie. She was unaware of Gertie and Grandpa at that moment. It was very quiet in the house, with just the click of Gertie's knitting needles and Grandpa's heavy breathing as background.

Then Gertie said, 'Shall we tell her our little secret, Ted?' Ted was Grandpa.

'It won't be no little secret if we tell her,' Grandpa said.

'She'll keep it to herself, won't you, lovie?'

'Will I?' Sandy looked up and saw Gertie's toothless grin widening over the top of her grey dishcloth. She had long hairs sticking out of her chin. Yet she did the Charleston once at Brankhead Hall. Sandy blinked.

'What is it?'

'You won't tell anyone? Not your mum or dad?'

'No.'

'When I go from here, I'm taking your grandad with me.'

For some reason – possibly because Grandpa had always been keen on saying that when he left Drakesend it would be in a box – Sandy thought Gertie was talking about dying.

'What's wrong with you? How can you take Grandpa?' A suicide pact? 'You're not going to do that!'

'Yes, we are. We're going together.'

'But—'

'We're going to get married.'

Sandy nearly passed out. She was speechless. Marriage was for young things: Glynn and Josie (although they hadn't got round to it), even Polly and Tony . . . She looked up, her brain jumbled with shock, and saw that the bead-bright eyes over the grey knitting were full of sparks. There was no other way of describing it. They danced, and in their light Sandy saw that yes, Gertie had kicked her legs to the Charleston, her slender, pretty legs before the old brown stockings had covered them, and yes, that bony pale skull had been thick with curls and that gaping smile full of pearly teeth. The old spirit shone through. Sandy could see it, suddenly.

'Just 'cause you look old, doesn't mean to say you feel old,' Gertie said. 'You'll remember that one day.'

Sandy felt a hundred and ten. Just because you look young, doesn't mean to say you feel young. She got up and gave Gertie a kiss. It was instinctive. She had never kissed Gertie before and would have said she would rather die.

'That's great, Gertie.'

'You're not to say anything!'

'No. It's a secret.'

'All in good time. That's a good girl.'

Sandy drifted out to the stable. She wanted fresh air. Where had her mother gone? What was her mother up to, with that awful look on her face, while Gertie and Grandpa were courting in the kitchen? Her head reeled.

Jonas was coming up the drive on Queen Moon.

'Hi, Sandy.'

Sandy's senses zoomed to a new high. She felt a ridiculous, goofy smile breaking through, a fierce blush firing her hairline. Everything else was forgotten.

'Jonas!'

'I came to see you. I want to ask you something.'

'Yes?'

Queen Moon came to a halt in front of her and Jonas slipped down. His gypsy smile was diffident, nervous.

'You said – you said you would take her, if I went away.'

'Queen Moon?'

'Yes.'

'Of course I will!'

He hesitated still, and Sandy raced in: 'You needn't pay, not if you can't. She can go down in the field, no trouble.'

'You mean that? It would be great.'

'When are you going?' Where? she wanted to scream. How long for? Why? Don't go!

'As soon as I get her fixed, I thought I'd go. I can't live with my father any longer. I want to see if I can get on a trawler. Anything, really, for my keep. I don't care. Away.'

'Of course I'll keep her for you. I'll look after her. She'll be fine here.'

'She'll like being out, a bit of grass.'

He held out the rope halter. Sandy took it.

She couldn't bear it, seeing him, and now he was going. It had taken barely a minute.

'You're going now?'

'I'll go home and collect a few things, then I'll be off, yes. I'll get a lift up on the main road.'

'If we put her in the field, I can walk along the sea-wall with you – a little way—'

'OK.'

He seemed agreeable, not embarrassed. Sandy turned Queen Moon out with Blackie and her yearling. The grey mare fell to grazing immediately and took no notice of Blackie's curiosity. There was no fighting or kicking. Sandy hung the halter on the gate.

'It was the only thing troubling me, the mare,' Jonas said. 'She'll be happy here.'

They walked together across the marsh fields towards the sea-wall, crossing the ditches which were full of wild marigolds and yellow aconites – the same ditches that the team-chasers had been practising on (funny, after all their practice, that there were hardly any plain ditches on the course they were going to ride). Sandy chattered on about the team to cover her nervous excitement, all the while feeling sick that he was going. The only good thing was having Queen Moon: he would come back to see her whenever – if ever – he came home, and Sandy knew she was included in the package. To see Queen Moon he would see her too. She kept stealing sideways glances at his loping figure beside her: he moved like a poacher, quietly and smoothly, and his voice was soft and secretive – he was like no-one else she knew. She told him about sleeping in the loft and the burglar coming again. He did not say anything and she remembered how, early on, he had been a prime suspect.

'It's horrid. I wish now—' Her voice trailed. Did she really want to know? Her mother had acted very strangely.

'Sometimes it's better to let things be,' Jonas said.

'Not to know?' Just what Duncan had said.

'If I were you,' Jonas said, 'I'd forget it.'

'You know who it is?'

Jonas did not reply. He shrugged his shoulders.

Sandy knew, then, where her mother had gone.

She stopped. 'I'm going back,' she said. 'I can't come all the way.'

'OK.' Jonas turned round and smiled.

The smile was all she had. She was going to hold on to it like grim death.

'Good luck, with the job.'

'If I get it.'

'You'll get what you want.'

'And you.'

She turned and started to hurry back, before he saw her crying. It was all terrible. Far away, from the farm, she heard Queen Moon whinny. But Jonas walked on, not looking back.

'It's Glynn, isn't it?'

Her mother swung round, with her sharp, anguished look. They were washing-up, and no-one else was in the kitchen.

'He won't do it any more! I've spoken to him, the stupid idiot! He's promised. For God's sake,

180

Sandy, don't say anything to a soul. We can get over it, we can forget it, as long as you don't breathe a word.'

Sandy was astonished.

'But what—'

'He's promised! It won't happen again.'

'Does Dad know?'

'No. Nobody knows.'

'They do! They don't say!' Sandy burst out, thinking of Duncan, of Jonas. 'It's not fair to have everyone suspected still, when you know who it is!'

'Sandy, have some sense! What would happen – their relationship, the baby— He's *promised* – he really has! He realizes what he would lose. He's just a stupid boy, too young for responsibility. They should never have had the child – how stupid can you get? It's all too much for him. But he'll pull himself together now, get a proper job. It will be all right.'

Had Glynn promised all that, in the hour that the shepherd's pie was browning? Sandy was shaken by her mother's attitude. She remembered, when Glynn had first been introduced to the family, how worried her parents had been by his devil-may-care attitude to life. Yet she had thought him wonderful, as Josie had – such fun, such a happy laugh, his witty remarks and jokes . . . no wonder Josie had loved him! Her parents said he didn't seem to have much ambition. 'Oh, he can do anything with his hands!' Josie exlaimed. Yes, it seemed, he could – lifting other people's property. He had tried to steal Ian's bike only the night before – his own friend's property!

'Mum, you can't not tell! Tell Dad, at least.'

'He's got enough worries, it would break him! You know how he adores Josie. He's tried really hard to get on good terms with Glynn and it has all been working – famously . . . ' Mary Fielding's voice gave way and she let out a hiccuping sob.

'Oh, Mum, don't!'

'You mustn't say anything, Sandy. Later, perhaps, but not just now. Give him another chance – give us all some breathing space. I will sort it out, I promise you.'

'Mum, you can't—' But a glance at her mother's face silenced her. Later perhaps. It did not all have to be resolved this minute, when her mother's face looked like that, and she was crying. In a day or two she would see sense. She was overwrought, had been for ages, driven demented by Gertie and all the extra work. But Gertie was going soon, back to her cottage with Grandpa. If her mother knew that—

'Mum, Gertie told me—' Sandy stopped in mid-sentence, remembering that it was a secret.

'Gertie doesn't know? How can she?' her mother snapped.

'No, of course not. It was something else. But it doesn't matter.'

Sandy longed to tell, but the sharp image of Gertie's glee stopped her. She, Sandy, was a keeper of secrets – Gertie's, Glynn's, her mother's. She wouldn't be able to speak to anyone, for fear of blurting out something she shouldn't. What could she tell Leo?

'I'm not sleeping in the loft any more. I'm coming back home.'

Her mother needed looking after, not the yard.

A large and very grand horsebox drove into the yard. Tony got out, looking very spruce in his birthday-present jacket, snowy breeches and shining boots.

'The great day!'

'Whoever did you borrow that lorry from?'

'It's Julia's. Julia's ma's. Didn't she tell you?'

'Really?'

No, Sandy didn't know that they were going to borrow the Marsden horsebox for the day. Surprise, surprise. (But she knew a few things none of the others knew.) She thought Julia might have told her, all the same.

'I thought you knew,' Julia said, when accosted. Sandy was in an accosting mood, very ratty.

'Well, I didn't.'

Sandy was glad she wasn't riding, because she could see that Leo was petrified with fear, but at the same time she was deeply jealous of the others. It didn't make sense. The conflict made her feel bad.

They weren't riding until mid-afternoon, so they had plenty of time to get ready. While the grooming and gear-collecting was going on, Sandy went down the field to talk to Queen Moon. Every day she took her down a feed, because she was too thin, and talked to her. She thought the mare was pining, because she did not graze for long periods, but stood in the far corner of the field looking towards Riverhead as if she thought Jonas would appear. Sandy knew he wouldn't. She felt much the same as Queen Moon and would stand with her arm round the mare's neck, talking to her. It made her feel better, but whether it made any difference to Queen Moon she could not tell. But the mare nuzzled her in a friendly fashion: the offer of affection was not rejected.

'Suppose he never comes back?' the others asked. 'Is she yours?'

'Of course he'll come back.'

Queen Moon could never be hers. She was a part of Jonas. Jonas had made her.

While Sandy was mooning down the field – they all called it 'mooning', her obsession with Queen Moon – Julia was grooming Faithful for the impending competition, still not quite sure what she thought about it. A quite large sliver of her was excited. Unlike the others, she wasn't nervous. After her upbringing in highly competitive show-jumping, she saw that bashing across country was much easier (on Faithful at least) and more fun, and with no onus 'to win' , only get round, the afternoon looked promising. She realized that they were all depending on her as the anchor-man, the only one who wasn't frightened of getting carted. Polly was the leader: she had worked out the tactics – as far as possible – but several times she had deferred to Julia, suggesting she might set the pace, or take the lead in the tricky places, always respectful of her ability. It made Julia feel really good. Her mother had always taken her ability for granted. Julia had rarely been praised: she was expected to win. That was the norm – taken for granted. Anything less and she had been reviled. After the whole winter with Faithful, Julia realized that she was getting her nerve back, and her enthusiasm, for so long stifled by fear, was gradually returning. It made her feel good, and more friendly than usual. This team business was interesting – quite different from bombing on to win on one's own. It was impossible to be a 'loner' under the circumstances.

When she led Faithful out to box her, Polly grimaced and said, 'She does look small beside the others. I bet there'll be an objection from someone or other.'

'Only if we win,' said Leo. 'And we won't.'

Leo was thinking her whole family could live in this horsebox – the living quarters were nearly as big as their sitting-room at home. It had a cooker, a fridge, a sink, a bar and a shower unit. And there was still room for four horses. They piled in their tack, their sweat-rugs, haynets, water buckets, hats, jerseys, grooming-boxes, sandwiches, schedules . . .

'I've left my leather jacket in the tackroom,' Tony remarked, as they were setting off up the lane. 'I hope that burglar's not in business this afternoon.'

'That's when we lost the saddles – when we were all out that night,' Polly said.

'You should go back for it,' Leo said.

'We're running a bit late,' Polly said.

'It won't get stolen,' Sandy said. 'It's all finished now.'

Leo shot her a very strange look, but did not say anything, and Sandy realized she had spoken tactlessly.

'Everyone else is at home,' she added quickly. 'Nobody's going to come in broad daylight.'

Tony drove as if he had been a long-distance lorry driver all his life, and they arrived at Aspen Farm in good order. It was a perfect spring day, sunny but with a keen wind, no sign of rain, and the horseboxes were lined up in droves. The familiar smell of hot dogs floated across the field; sweaty horses were coming back up the hill, heads down, riders laughing and breathless, and others, cool and keen, were being led out ready to go, their riders tying on numbers. Ladies in green quilted jackets with golden retrievers on leads chatted with tweeded men who raised their caps politely, and the Young Farmers were bulging out of the beer tent as usual. It was a scene perfectly familiar to Polly and Sandy and Julia, but it made Leo feel sick, and Tony was rather quiet.

Polly said to him softly, 'You've got the best horse of the lot. Don't be put off.'

At last, Sandy thought, he realizes he's not much of a rider. But she felt sympathetic towards him. He really had improved since knowing them. The only one without a horse, Sandy was the fetcher and carrier: 'Hold this, hold that. What's the time? Where's the hoofpick? Get our numbers, there's a darling.' Julia and Polly knew the drill, but Tony had to be helped, and Leo was in a panic. It was all confusion. While they were working against the clock, their various parents came to visit – Tony's mother looking as if she expected to lead in the Gold Cup winner at Cheltenham; Julia's tight-lipped and critical – 'We've given up a day's jumping for you to do this, Julia. I hope it will be worth it.'

'I never asked you to,' Julia said.

'I'm curious to see what you do with your time, that's all.'

Sandy, watching, thought what rotten luck they both had with their mothers. Leo's boffin pair were not there. They didn't approve of bloodsports. Leo had told them it wasn't bloodsports and they said, 'What are you chasing then?' Leo was relieved to be panicking in private. 'God, Sandy, I'm petrified!'

'Once you start, you'll be fine,' Sandy said briskly, hoping it was true. More petrified, probably. But Leo needed stiffening. Polly gave her something out of a bottle. Somehow they all got mounted and numbered and down the hill in the direction of the start.

King of the Fireworks went as if he had seen it all before, as no doubt he had – interested and alert, but calm. Charlie's Flying knew what he had to do and couldn't wait, fighting and charging about like a naughty pony. Polly had got him very cheap for quite obvious reasons. Empress of China was looking very surprised and slightly suspicious, not quite sure if she was on a racecourse again, and Faithful was living up to her name: willing and obedient and perfect.

There was a place in the middle of the course from where one could see most of the action apart from what went on in the wood, and Sandy had decided to go up there. It was at the top of the long grass field out of the wood, near the pen, and at the back of her mind she thought she might be useful if any of them couldn't stop – exactly how, she hadn't decided. Running down the field waving her arms probably wouldn't result in anything more than getting run down. But it was a gesture. As she turned to make her way in that direction she saw Ian on his mountain bike, cycling towards her. She was amazed.

'What are you doing here?'

'I thought it might be a laugh.'

'You could have come in the horsebox.'

'I didn't want to come *that* badly,' he said rudely.

Sandy wondered if he still liked Julia. Perhaps that was why he had come.

'They're up by the start. There's three to go before them. I was going to watch by that tree.'

'OK.' He got off and pushed his bike beside her.

'Why aren't you in the team?'

'Leo's better than me.'

When they were together, doing something, not just moping round the house, they seemed to get on quite well. Sandy remembered good days making camps and fishing and showing the farm dog in a dog show and going to a football match, when they had once got on like good mates. Now, after his initial rudeness, Ian seemed quite human and interested and made her think of those times. If only he was always . . . Oh, why couldn't she *talk* to him! What good was a brother like Ian? Suddenly breathless, heart thumping, she said, 'The burglar came again last week – in the night. Did Mum tell you?'

He turned to her sharply. She saw quite suddenly that he wasn't a boy any longer, but had a man's face. He looked quite different.

'Did you see him?'

'No. But I know who it is.'

He did not reply. They walked together across the tussocky grass and watched a team coming up the field towards them, hell for leather, the riders shouting to each other. They detoured, and gained the safety of the hedgerow. The team milled round the pen, getting in each other's way. One member was still only just coming out of the wood, and the first horse jumped out before the last came in through the slip-rail. He had to come round and go in again. They were all shouting and screaming at each other. Sandy, watching, waited for Ian to say something, but he didn't. They got to the hedgerow and stood under an oak tree. Ian leaned his bike against it.

'Do you know who it is?' Sandy persisted.

'I've got a good idea.'

'Who?'

He didn't reply. He looked at her with eyes which were exactly the same as Josie's – very cool.

'It's Glynn,' Sandy said. She waited. 'Is that who you thought?' she persisted.

He nodded.

'Mum knows, but she won't do anything about it. She's got to!'

'Why?'

'He came again three nights ago, to pinch your

bike. I screamed and he ran away. I told Mum and she says don't tell anybody, not even Dad. She went down to see him, I think.'

She could see that Ian was jolted by nearly losing his bike.

'I wouldn't have thought he'd take my bike!'

'It's no worse than the saddles. How can Mum not say?'

'Mum's in a state.'

'I know.' But so am I, Sandy wanted to say. 'She's acting in a funny way. I think Dad ought to know. He's got to know sooner or later. Will you tell him?'

'But if Glynn doesn't do it any more, if Mum's spoken to him, it could be finished now. He isn't that stupid, is he?'

'Fairly, I think, to keep doing it on his own doorstep. The trouble is, if people don't know, they might think it could be – well, Duncan, or – or Jonas – or—' She nearly said 'you', but didn't.

'But if it's finished, people forget.'

Ian looked a bit saggy, like his mother. He said, 'It's – it's Josie who worries me, really. I've kept out of it, kept my head down. After the saddles went, Glynn had a roll of notes and Josie was surprised. I noticed. She said, "Wherever did you get that from?" and he said he'd done a job, but he was worried, I could see. Because I was there. It just struck me, he looked really scared. He changed the subject very quickly. Josie said, "I didn't know

192

the jobs you did were so well paid!" It made her happy, she made jokes about it, and he got cross suddenly and told her not to be so – well, he swore at her. I was embarrassed. It was then that I thought – well – it struck me. It was horrible.'

'What, after the saddles went . . . you've known ages?'

'Not known. Just wondered.'

'I thought it was Duncan. Because I found his penknife in Gertie's drive.'

'Duncan!'

'Yes. That's what I mean. When you don't know, you suspect all sorts of people.'

'Well, if Mum's had a go at Glynn . . . he won't do it again, surely? He wouldn't be so daft.'

'You want to keep quiet, like Mum?'

'I'd rather, yes. Because of Josie. But it's – it's—' He swore. He looked quite different from the usual closed-up Ian. He looked human and concerned. Sandy suddenly saw that he might turn out quite nice in the end.

'Will you talk to Mum about it? Please!' Sandy blurted out. It wouldn't be so bad if it wasn't all her responsibility. It was much better already, talking about it. 'I can't bear thinking about it all by myself, and Mum being so – so odd.' Unmotherish.

'Would it help?'

'It would help me! I think it would help her too, if we all talked about it – Dad as well. She's trying to keep it secret and it's killing her.'

Just at this vital stage of the conversation she saw that the Drakesend team was about to start. Charlie's Flying seemed to be wanting to go the wrong way, but as far as Sandy could judge, Polly was shouting to the others to set off, in the hope that he would then decide to join his friends. Julia obliged by setting off for the first jump at a brisk pace, and King of the Fireworks lobbed after her, followed by a rather hesitant Empress of China.

Sandy's domestic problems were forgotten instantly. She was as one with Leo approaching the first tiger-trap over the ditch, feeling the old mare's surprise and lack of enthusiasm. Far from wanting to bolt, she wanted to go back to the horsebox. Polly was miles behind, but at least now had Charlie's Flying facing in the right direction. Seeing his departing friends, he shot forward like a bullet.

King of the Fireworks' long stride brought him up level with Faithful, and the large horse and the pony jumped side by side, in textbook fashion. Not so textbook behind them, Empress of China refused, switching round sideways and presenting herself side on to fast-approaching Charlie's Flying. Too late to pull up, he crashed into the Empress, knocking her half into the ditch. Leo and Polly clashed knees painfully, but neither fell off and both emerged from the fracas none the worse for wear, pointing back towards the start. Polly made a fair-sized circle, shouting, 'Keep close behind me!' and pointed Charlie at the jump again. He flew it and this time the Empress made a grudging leap in pursuit and they both landed safely on the other side.

Julia had trotted up the long field to allow the pair behind to catch up, and King of the Fireworks had kept with her, but with the advent of wild Charlie and a rejuvenated Empress, the two in front speeded up. King of the Fireworks reached out, lengthening his stride, and went straight past little Faithful, even though she was now galloping. Polly had got Charlie back in control, and they approached the well-named coffin spread out in a line. Tony hadn't the experience to steady his horse for the jump, but clever Fireworks knew exactly what was wanted and went through the complex like a cat. Three jumps, one after the other, and Tony by the end had lost his stirrups, his reins and his cool, and disappeared into the trees with a cry of despair. Faithful followed, and Polly, having wrestled Charlie almost to a halt, managed to get a very neat performance at the jump. The Empress, obviously afraid to be left on her own, flew after him.

'Tony's going to fall off!' Sandy moaned.

He wasn't meant to be in front through the wood. Anything could happen in there.

'That horse of Polly's is a maniac,' Ian remarked, truly.

'At least she can ride – not like Tony!'

They waited for what seemed eternity for the team to reappear. At least no signals were sent for the ambulance, which remained somnolent up by the start. At last there was a flash of movement and the lean chestnut shape of Empress of China shot out of the trees, up the bank and into the field and set off hell for leather for home before any of the others had even appeared.

'Leo!' Sandy wailed.

This was where one had to jump, turn and neatly jump back into the wood. The Empress didn't know about this, only that she didn't like woods and wanted to go home. As she approached at a flat gallop the spot where Sandy and Ian were standing, Sandy could see Leo hauling with all her strength on the hard old mouth to get the mare to circle back. As there was a thick hedge ahead of her, she was partially successful. Sandy saw Leo's face, white as a sheet, blur past. Ian was laughing his head off.

'Is this competition serious?' he asked.

Sandy did not deign to reply. It was deadly serious for Leo, she reckoned. But Leo's panic had produced the strength to haul the old mare back on course, and as she found herself alone again, with nowhere to go, she slowed down, dropping back into a trot. Finding herself alone, she let out a resounding whinny. Leo turned her round and at the bottom of the long field she saw her three friends waiting for her, having emerged one by one out of the wood. As far as Sandy could see, they were all in one piece – even Tony.

Neighing in a highly unprofessional manner, the chestnut mare cantered back to the team, and Julia, at a shout from Polly, turned Faithful to jump back into the wood again. This she did very neatly, followed by the other two. Empress of China, directed towards the jump, remembered that she didn't like woods, lost impulsion and refused. Leo had thought she would jump and shot up round the mare's ears, but luckily the old girl didn't put her head down and Leo was able to push herself back into the saddle. She circled again and, legs crashing wildly against the mare's sides, she persuaded her to take a poky cat-leap over the bar into the wood. It looked anything but fluent and heart-lifting, but it got her to the other side where the others were apparently waiting, for none of them had appeared yet out of the wood for the second time.

In retrospect, it might have helped if they had carried on and come out of the wood and up the big field to the pen one by one, rather than in a bunch. Having been held up, the other three horses were now all eager to get on with it. They jumped out on each others' heels, Faithful leading, and Empress of China, last, jumped this time with such abandon she landed alongside Charlie's Flying. This obviously stirred her old racing instincts for she immediately went away at a gallop none of them knew was in her, outstripping even the long-striding King of the Fireworks. For the second time she streaked up the field towards Sandy and Ian, putting lengths between herself and the rest of the team.

Sandy groaned and shut her eyes, feeling Leo's panic flaring in her own breast. And to think she had wanted the ride herself! Leo had no option but to try and circle again. Tony was trying hard not to follow her on King of the Fireworks, but without success. Faithful went neatly and obediently into the pen, and Polly managed to get Charlie in as well, and there they had to wait while the other two members of their team careered round the countryside, trying to regain control. Sandy thought the Empress was likely to drop dead as she was by now lathered with sweat – who would tell Uncle Arthur?

'Funny old sport, this,' Ian commented. 'I'm not surprised they don't do it on television.'

'It's more interesting than snooker,' Sandy snapped.

Eventually, by the time Leo was as exhausted as the mare, they managed to converge on the pen. Tony had got there shortly before them, and as Empress of China, reunited with her friends again, passed through the gateway, Julia slipped the rail back into place. By the time she had remounted, Polly was away over the rail and off up the next field, followed by the three others.

Sandy breathed a sigh of relief. The worst was over, she hoped. They were heading for home now and, hopefully, tiring.

Over the next stretch it was Faithful who got left behind, the big horses shooting past, but at the next ditch but one, Tony fell off. King of the Fireworks jumped very big, a stride before Tony was expecting, and Tony was dumped in the water. Polly caught Fireworks who – typically, and unlike Charlie or the Empress – thought it good manners to wait for a fallen rider, and Tony scrambled aboard again. By this time, Faithful had caught up and they rode very respectably, all together like a proper team, round the bottom of the course and over another ditch and rail. Nobody fell off and nobody was now bolting. Only the long uphill to the finish was left, with one easy fence on the way.

Here King of the Fireworks came into his own, striding powerfully round the bottom bend and pulling hard as he came up the hill. He took the fence in his stride and showed no signs of tiring – nor of stopping either. Charlie's Flying chased him hard, Polly driving him on, grinning like a monkey, and behind them brilliant little Faithful was coming as fast as her lack of inches allowed. Leo, on the Empress, knowing that their score was decided by the first three horses home, eased up and came up the hill at a mere trot. The chestnut mare was covered in lather and breathing hard, but there was a heady light in her eyes. Leo, slumped exhausted over her neck, cried out to Sandy, 'Oh, she was marvellous! She loved it! It was wonderful!'

'You could have fooled me,' Ian said.

Leo slithered to the ground. She could hardly stand up. Sandy ran and took the reins of the excited mare.

'It was great! You all made it! Good old Empress!' She patted the dripping neck, infected now with Leo's euphoria. They had all got round, for better or for worse, and now it was over there was a heady sense of achievement. Polly rode back, grinning all over her face.

'King of the Fireworks hasn't stopped yet. He went through the gate and looks set to go round again. Poor old Tony!'

They all trailed up the hill back to the horse-boxes. Julia came behind on Faithful who was still as fresh as paint. She had done a faultless round. Julia's mother was waiting for her.

'That pony's not bad – if you got together with a decent bunch, you could be up with the winners.'

'I like this bunch,' Julia said.

Her mother rolled her eyes. 'They—'

'Oh, shut up,' said Julia.

The Marsdens were incredibly rude to each other, Sandy thought. But Mrs Marsden didn't take it amiss.

'We'll get you a bigger animal. She's too small. She must be worth a bit, now you've got her jumping ironed out.'

'She's mine. I'm not selling her. I'm small too, or haven't you noticed?'

While this bickering was going on, Tony's mother was waiting for them, fluffed up with concern like a broody bantam.

'Is he all right? Surely this is all very dangerous? Where is he?'

'He likes it so much he's doing it again,' Polly said.

She wasn't too concerned: King of the Fireworks was such a Christian beast that she did not think Tony would come to any harm, even when he was out of control. What a horse! And yet Tony, knowing no other, took him completely for granted. Polly had paid a mere five hundred pounds for Charlie's Flying because no-one else could ride him (and live), yet Tony had been *given* a horse worth ten thousand pounds at least and didn't have an inkling of what a treasure he possessed. King of the Fireworks was king of far more than fireworks, and had a sweet and noble nature to go with his fabulous talent. If Polly had had an envious nature she would not have been able to cope with her feelings but, as

201

it was, getting Charlie's Flying round and merely coming home in one piece gave her the same wild elation that Leo had revealed.

'It was fabulous! Fantastic!'

Tony could be seen homing in on the horse-box from the far countryside.

'The old fool wanted to go round again!' he complained. But the common elation was evident beneath his soaked and muddy person. His blue eyes positively glowed.

'We did brilliantly!' Polly cried. 'You were all marvellous!'

'If that was brilliant,' Ian murmured to Sandy, 'what happens when everything goes wrong?'

'It feels brilliant, she means.'

'Because it's over?'

'On, shut up.'

They all had their hands full, unsaddling and cleaning up the horses. The team-chase was scored by time only, and their time on the board was about four times longer than the fastest, but they had completed.

'We got round!' Tony was carolling. 'Were you watching, Auntie?' he shouted to the heavens.

'Turning in her grave, I should imagine,' Ian said.

'Next time—' said Polly.

'Oh no!' Leo cried. 'Not again!'

They laughed and gabbled, still on a high. Sandy, helping, felt cut off. She could only guess how Leo felt now that it was over, having seen how terrified she had been. Did she really envy her? Sandy was confused, not knowing, but very much aware of her isolation. She had a sudden, hopeless dream of doing this competition on a perfect horse, her own horse, riding for her life and meeting jump after jump fluent and footsure, and riding up the hill with all the sky to meet her and the sun shining. The perfect horse – Queen Moon! But she knew it was never going to happen.

She was quiet as they drove home, but none of the others noticed. They were all screaming and laughing and recapping on the horrors of the day. Ian had departed on his mountain bike, declining a lift, and the two mothers had been left fraternizing, an unlikely pair, by the jacket-potato van.

When they got home, Sandy left them all to it. They had had the fun; they could do the work.

She had never been aware of this sort of envy before, not even sure if that was what it was. But suddenly it seemed, in face of that elated cohesion she had sensed in the others as they straggled back to the horsebox, that she had no share in what really mattered at all. She knew it was a passing depression in the direct aftermath of all the excitement, but in essence it was all part of the great confusion she felt wrapped up in. Who did you trust? Where were you going? What was it all about? Didn't any of the others feel like this sometimes?

Of course, most of the time, she didn't . . . just sometimes, when everyone else seemed to get it right and she was left on the sidelines.

She wanted to be on her own. She walked down the track out of the yard to the field gate where she could see Queen Moon grazing with Blackie and the yearling. The wind had dropped and the late sun was slanting down through the woods behind her, turning the high tide to a shimmering rose highway. The gulls dipped and squawked across the wall, and six shelduck were idling in the bottom field. Queen Moon set off the idyllic scene, her long shadow following her as she cropped the new grass.

Sandy called her and she came up obediently. She pushed her soft muzzle into Sandy's hand, although there was nothing in it, and stood quietly – possibly affectionately. It was hard to tell with a horse. She had the most beautiful head Sandy had ever seen in any horse – and that included King of the Fireworks; her eyes were huge and soft like an Arab's, and the outline of her nostrils made a bold and elegant curve. Her ears were long and forever attentive.

'I do love you!' Sandy whispered.

And Jonas too, but Jonas was gone. He would need money, and come back to sell Queen Moon. He had made her such a schooled ride that she was worth a good deal now. He would find her a good home without any trouble. Possibly someone might buy her and keep her at Drakesend. Perhaps Julia? Sandy wondered if she could persuade her.

Her summer coat was coming through, a deeper grey than the winter coat. Although she had been considered too small to race, she was not in any way spindly; she had a deep girth and was very compact. Since she had been at Drakesend she had filled out and looked much better. The freedom and the good grass agreed with her. Soon she would get too fat.

'When it gets hot you can come in during the day,' Sandy promised her. She would get the best. Graze in the cool of the night under her namesake, the summer moon. Nothing was too good for her.

Sandy walked back to the stable, comforted. Polly and Julia had gone. Only Tony was still there, about to depart in the impressive horsebox. He had a stupid grin on his face and seemed to be in a trance.

'I really enjoyed that,' he said. 'I didn't know – I've never—' Words seemed to fail him. 'I mean, I can see now that I – I'm not good enough for him.'

Sandy wished she had a tape recorder to immortalize these incredible words. Without it, Polly and Leo would never believe he had uttered them.

Contact with a great horse had improved him out of all measure. Would his devoted mummy notice the change?

'You are! At least you will be, now you see what it's all about. Now you realize—'

'It must take years to learn to ride like that – like Polly.'

'Yes. But you've got such a super horse. He's not difficult like Charlie. He will do it for you as long as you don't interfere with him.'

'I fell off, and he didn't do anything wrong.'

'But it was the first time – you'll get the hang of it.'

'It must be fantastic – racing – jumping—'

They all had their dreams. Tony climbed up into the cab and then remembered his leather jacket.

'I'll go and get it,' Sandy said, 'while you turn round.'

She went back to the tackroom, smiling at Tony's turn-around. It was hardly six months since he had arrived, so brash and revolting.

But the jacket had vanished.

11

'Go home, Tony. I know where it is. It'll be here tomorrow, I promise.'

What else could she say? She was committed now. It all had to be brought out into the open, whatever her mother thought.

Tony drove off, slightly puzzled but still more occupied with his momentous afternoon than with his material possessions, and Sandy waited for Ian. Her parents were out; she didn't know where.

'Oh, come on, come on!' she moaned, hopping from one foot to the other. All her moody thoughts were now swamped by this new horror. If this was solved, she would be brilliantly happy. Nothing else mattered at all. Her conversation with Ian earlier was now going to prove useful: he was clued up and was going to help her. She didn't think she could cope with it on her own any more.

She felt she had waited for an hour by the time he came down the drive, although in fact it was only ten minutes. She threw the news at him as soon as he was in earshot.

'What shall we do?'

To her great relief, he did not shrug it off or try to belittle it.

'That's terrible!'

They tried to think that it might be someone else, but in their hearts they thought it highly unlikely. Sandy made a thorough search of the tackroom, under the rugs and in the cupboards, but the jacket did not come to light.

'Let's go over there,' Ian said suddenly. 'Talk to Josie. Before Mum and Dad come home.'

'Oh yes!'

Anything to have it in the open, the miserable business solved. Sandy had a bike too, an ancient machine no-one would ever want to steal, which lived at the back of the haybarn. The quickest way to the Elizabethan tower was along the ancient driveway across the water-meadows. Grazed almost bare, it was flat and direct and perfect for bicycling. They set off purposefully, not saying anything. The sun had now disappeared behind the woody ridge above them and the only sound was of the rooks settling down in their rackety nests, ink blots against the orange sky. In half an hour it would be dark.

As they approached the tower, they saw the greenish light of a pressure lamp starring the kitchen window. Glynn's Land Rover was parked in its usual place on the driveway that led up to the road. Sandy had been hoping Josie would be alone.

Ian said softly, 'Let's look in the Land Rover. If he took it and doesn't want Josie to know, it might still be in there.'

Feeling like thieves themselves, they laid their bikes in the hedge and padded across the lawn to the Land Rover. There was nothing on the front seat. Ian climbed in the back, which was cluttered with tools, sacks, bits of timber and old diesel cans, and rooted around. Sandy couldn't see in the dusk, but could hear her heart thumping uneasily as she waited. Without proof on their part, Glynn could talk himself out of it, after all. Perhaps it was all wrong, what they were doing.

'Ian—' she started.

'Hush!'

He was backing out. He turned and lifted his legs over the tail-gate.

'Here.'

He threw something heavy and smooth into her arms. It was the leather jacket.

'It was under some sacks.'

It was a great relief, in spite of confirming her fears. Sandy could see that Ian felt the same, his chin lifting, his eyes sparking.

'We'll get him now.'

The satisfaction was momentary. Opening the

door, going in with the leather jacket over Sandy's arm, was dreadful.

Josie did not know the significance of it, but turned, smiling with surprise and welcome.

'Why, Ian! Sandy! How lovely! What's this in aid of?'

They hadn't visited often, after all, and never together that Sandy could remember. Josie was sitting at the table, spooning boiled egg into Selina's mouth which was poised, open, like a baby sparrow's beak, as Josie spoke. Glynn was just pouring out two cups of tea from the teapot. The newly lit lamp hissed on the end of the table and the fraint fragrance of woodsmoke hung in the room. It was a happy domestic scene.

Neither Ian nor Sandy found they could say anything. Sandy found herself making a weak gesture with the jacket. She saw instantly that Glynn knew what was up, but Josie said cheerfully, 'You've timed it well. Get another couple of mugs. There's plenty of tea in the pot. How did the competition go, Sandy? Mum was telling me all about it. I hope you won!'

'No fear,' said Sandy blankly.

'What's wrong? No accidents, I hope?'

'Oh, no. They all got round. It was OK.'

Josie looked blank suddenly, her welcome freezing.

'What's happened? Mum and Dad—?'

'They're OK. Fine.'

'Look, Glynn. This is Anthony Speerwell's.'

Ian took the jacket off Sandy and held it out.

'He missed it. We came to look, and there – well, we thought it might be . . . in your Land Rover.'

'Oh, God!' said Josie.

Glynn grinned. 'I didn't think he'd miss it, the gear he's got.'

'Glynn! The saddles!' Sandy cried out. 'Polly and Henry – *they* couldn't afford it!'

'And Gertie's savings!' Ian said.

'I *borrowed* Gertie's savings,' Glynn said. 'I'm going to pay Gertie back, I swear I will! The others – well, the insurance pays—'

They all stood looking at each other, very tense.

'You said you wouldn't, ever again – you said, Glynn!' Josie cried out in an agonized voice. 'You promised!'

'People leave things lying around—'

'You came for Ian's bike in the middle of the night, and unlocked the door. That's not things lying about!' Sandy shouted at him.

'Oh, he didn't!' Josie said faintly. 'You didn't do that, Glynn?'

'Well . . . look, we can talk about this,' Glynn said. 'Let's sit down and talk about it.'

'You're not going to the police? You haven't told them?' Josie whispered.

'No, we haven't told anybody, not even Mum and Dad,' Ian said.

'But Mum knows, I'm sure of it.' Sandy wanted Glynn to know — she *hated* him, standing there smiling, as if it were a joke.

'She asked me,' Josie said.

'And what did you say to her?' Glynn asked roughly. 'You told her it was true, I suppose?'

'I didn't! I never knew, did I? I never guessed — well, I didn't want to believe — perhaps—'

Sandy could see now that there was another side to Glynn, his natural exuberance tipping over into a bullying anger. He was a very large man, and Sandy had only seen him apparently gentle and smiling before. He now appeared extremely threatening.

The baby, Selina, sensing the atmosphere, started to cry. Josie lifted her out of her high chair and hugged her, hiding her face against the baby's soft body. She turned away and went and stood by the window, looking out into the dusk. Glynn watched her, and seemed to visibly soften, anxiety and distress smothering the anger. He looked at Ian and shrugged.

'Well, what are you going to do about it? Give him back his jacket — you can tell him where you found it. I don't care.'

Ian didn't know what to say. Sandy could see that there were no answers, in fact. She felt agonized for Josie, to whom it was more than just a few missing goods. It was Josie's life, linked to this man.

She sat down at the table. It was awful.

Ian whispered to her, 'I think we ought to go.'

'I'll give the jacket back to Tony. I won't tell him,' Sandy said to Glynn. It was the most she could do. 'But you said – you promise?'

'I swear to you,' Glynn said – the old Glynn, blond and bland and shining. His blue eyes were honest as the day.

There was a long silence. Sandy stood up and looked at Ian.

'We'll go,' Ian said. He picked up the jacket.

Josie lifted her head. 'Will you tell anyone?'

'No. It's up to you.'

'Mum knows,' Josie said. 'You can talk to her.' Her voice was a whisper.

Sandy couldn't bear it. She blundered out of the door and into the garden, and Ian came after her. He put Tony's jacket on and pulled his bike out of the hedge. Sandy picked up hers. They walked out and shut the gate and started home along the smooth carriageway. The sun had disappeared, but the sky was still orange over the ridge and the sky above a deep velvet blue. It was a beautiful evening but, deeply disturbed, they couldn't see it. Sandy, trying to look on the bright side, said eventually, 'At least it's wonderful to know – stop guessing. Worrying.' Pretty awful about who it was though.

'Apart from Gertie's savings – well, I suppose

pinching things – it's not all that dreadful.'

'From your own family it's pretty dreadful,' Sandy couldn't help saying.

'It's not violent. Just mean.'

'Yes. Mean.'

How could he, Sandy wondered? Those treasured saddles. Ian's bike.

'We'll tell Tony that Mum put the jacket in the house, for safety,' she said.

They pedalled slowly home, not saying any more. The best thing, Sandy thought, was being in accord with Ian – the first time she had felt this for ages. She hadn't realized how apart they had become. She would have hated to confront Glynn on her own, yet she couldn't have let it ride, even if Ian hadn't wanted to know. But he had been solid, dependable. She glanced at him sideways, in the dusk. It was true that he seemed suddenly older. Perhaps he would be all right now, if Gertie went away with Grandpa and their mother stopped getting so uptight. Perhaps everything wasn't so awful after all. In the great scheme of things, Glynn being light-fingered wasn't much to make a song and dance about.

She felt a lot better, thinking this. There was a wonderful smell of spring and the first stars were coming out over the sea.

'There, Gertie, what do you think?'

Sandy opened the door into the living-room

of the small cottage. She and Ian between them had papered the walls with a lovely paper – old-fashioned, with daisies all over it. It was their wedding present. Some of the corners were a bit uneven, but the pattern was so fussy the mistakes didn't show much. It had taken them a whole weekend, Sandy pasting and Ian up the ladder. They hadn't argued much and had found great satisfaction in the result.

'It's lovely, isn't it?' Sandy thought it was, anyway.

'Oh, my word, yes!'

Gertie stood there smiling. After all these weeks of sitting doing nothing, she had walked down the drive and up the lane to her cottage like a Trojan, as if her strength had been conserved. The boiler in the kitchen had been lit for a week and the place was inviting and homely, scrubbed and polished, the curtains all washed, the fire laid in the grate. They had never dreamed at Drakesend that it was really going to happen, but with the first spring sunshine Gertie had stirred out of hibernation.

'It'll be good to come home, dearie. So pretty you've made it! If your mother hadn't needed me, I'd have been back long ago. But I didn't want her to think I was ungrateful.'

Sandy gawped. Gertie went round touching all her furniture, putting her ornaments in the right position, smoothing the cushions.

'Very nice. Very nice indeed.'

'Do you want to stay? We've filled the pantry. It only needs bread and veg and things – we've thought of everything. Lots of tins and that. It's all ready. I can go and get bread now if you like.'

'Tomorrow, dear. I'll come tomorrow.'

Would she? They walked home together. Gertie had a stick, but did not falter. She was smiling. When they got back to the farm she said, 'I'll go and pack my things,' and went upstairs.

'I'm not sure if I believe this,' Mary Fielding said to Sandy.

'She said she only stayed because you needed her.'

'Oh!'

Sandy grinned.

Mary said, 'It's dreadful, how selfish we all are. How badly we've behaved over Gertie. I'm the worst.'

'You did everything for her!'

'But I resented it all the time! Everything that wasn't her fault – Ian being so bloody-minded, the worry over Glynn and Josie – I snapped at her. I took it out on Gertie.'

'Oh, Mum, she was pretty annoying! Never helping or anything. Hogging the television. Don't be daft!'

'It's been a bad time, I suppose – Glynn . . . awful. All coming together.'

'It's all right now, surely? Josie says it's all right.'

'Josie's a great one for dreams! But she's strong. With luck she'll make him see sense. We told her to wait when she fell in love, but no – she knew it all, didn't she? Glynn wants everything too easy – the idea of a job, eight to five, always frightened him to death. But now – now he must buckle down.'

'Oh, Mum! He will! Josie will make him!'

'Yes. She's strong. Let's hope so.'

'You've got the wedding to fix next!'

None of them quite knew what to think about the wedding, whether it was touching or potty or a big mistake. Gertie had been married before but she had no children. There was no-one, really, to suffer any repercussions whether it turned out well or badly. It was to be at Easter, and just about everybody in the county over the age of seventy was expecting an invitation. Grandpa was selling the family heirlooms to pay for it: a gold pocketwatch, his first wife's pearl necklace, and an old picture of a horse lying down in a field, by George Morland. Sandy rather liked the horse, which had hung in the old study ever since she could remember, but no doubt the wedding would give more pleasure. The picture turned out to be quite valuable.

'Quite a few thousand, would you believe!'

They all scrubbed round to see if there was anything else they might have overlooked, but no . . . only the furniture, which they used. It was antique and no doubt valuable, but it belonged there. It had always been there.

'No shortcuts! We've just got to work for our dosh,' Mary said with a sigh.

With Gertie and Grandpa going and all that work about to evaporate, she had arranged to use her spare time to make quiches for a local pub. She was a good cook and was quite excited about her new venture.

'Perhaps Josie can come in too, and make some extra cash. Keep Glynn out of mischief.'

'Will he be OK now? You've talked to him?'

'They want a tractor driver up at Endway and he could do that – your father's spoken to them and they say they'll give him a trial. So that might work out.'

At last, Sandy gave Duncan his penknife back. She told him where she had found it and how it had worried her, and Duncan said, 'Aye, it worried me too. I called on Gertie that night, to fix a washer for her on the kitchen tap, and afterwards I couldn't find my knife. I thought maybe it was in her kitchen – evidence, like. I told the police I'd been there, naturally, so if they found it—' He shrugged, grinned. 'So you had it all the time. You didn't say?'

Sandy felt herself going scarlet with shame. 'I didn't want it to be you! I daren't ask! That was what was so horrid about it all the time. Sometimes I thought it was Ian.'

Duncan laughed. He was one of the best, self-effacing and kind, and had not split on Glynn, even when he knew.

'It was hard,' he said, 'but I reckoned it was a family thing. I saw him in the tackroom the time the money went missing. It wasn't for me to say.' The others in the yard were too busy thinking of team-chasing to remember the burglaries. The insurance had paid out on the saddles, and only Leo knew about the night of Ian's bike. She never asked Sandy any more about who it might have been, and Sandy suspected she did not ask on purpose, because she guessed. Leo was very bright.

The nights were warm, the grass was growing fast, and at last the horses could be turned out. Sandy loved the coming of summer and the easing of her workload. Tony, at last, was beginning to do-it-himself, coming over early to exercise and groom and feed so that his horse would be fit to compete, and it was obvious that he was doing it not just for his great-aunt's money, but because the competition bug had bitten. He was besotted by galloping across country. King of the Fireworks had made a man of him, just as his old hunting auntie had intended.

As for the rest of the team, it was in a state of ferment most of the time – Leo deciding she never wanted to do it again, then changing her mind; Julia declaring she hated competing; and Polly wondering if she might get killed if she persisted.

To Sandy, without a horse, it was academic. Life was like that, she had discovered – highs and lows. One took a chance or settled for the safe and the dull, or perhaps had no choice.

She took to going down to talk to Queen Moon, who came to the gate when she saw her coming. Queen Moon now had her summer coat and she had put on weight. Her ribs barely showed. Sandy was hoping that the mare was transferring her rapport with Jonas to herself; certainly she looked for her coming and showed her affection. Leo said she ought to ride her, but Sandy felt there was no way she could do that without Jonas's permission. She thought that Leo was hoping Queen Moon could take the Empress's place in the Drakesend Dodderers. Leo had professed herself too scared to ever ride again, but no-one was taking her seriously, except Sandy. Sandy did not dare comment, the idea of riding Queen Moon in the team too glorious to contemplate. If only Jonas would come back! There was no word of him, and even his father, Tony reported, had no idea of his whereabouts.

'Suppose he never comes back?' Leo asked. 'What will you do then?'

'Die,' said Sandy, to fob her off.

She stood in her bedroom window and pressed her nose against the pane. It seemed an age since she had watched for 'the wild boy' on the silver horse, galloping along the sea-wall in the moon-light. How romantic it had seemed then – and still did, in spite of the fact that the wild boy was now probably working on an oil-rig or gutting fish on a trawler. Sandy didn't think she would see him again.

Afterwards, she sometimes wondered if she dreamed what happened next. Everything to do with Jonas was a dream, after all, except the party. It was hard to know fact from fiction, save that Queen Moon grazed in her field down by the river.

There was a figure on the sea-wall, not galloping but walking. A fast, easy, gypsy pace, coming from the direction of Brankhead. Queen Moon put her head up and whinnied. Even through the glass, Sandy heard the whinny. The boy ran towards her and the mare trotted down the field to meet him.

'He's come to take her away!'

Sandy let out a loud, despairing sob. She stood frozen, trembling with love and despair.

The boy put his arms round the mare's neck, but did not vault on as Sandy was expecting. He gave her a hug, then stood back as if to examine her, but she turned round, nuzzling him. He hugged her again. He gave her titbits from his pockets. He put his hand on her neck and walked to the gate with her. But he did not go through. He sat on the gate and seemed to be talking to her.

Afterwards, Sandy supposed that if she had run fast enough she would have caught him before he went. But she seemed to be made of lead, fastened to the floor. The tears rolled down her cheeks. He went away the way he had come, and when the mare couldn't follow him because of the fence, she stood and whinnied, looking after him. Jonas didn't turn round. He ran. Perhaps he was crying too?

Sandy waited. A long time after Jonas disappeared, Queen Moon started to graze again. Occasionally, she lifted her head and looked towards Brankhead, but soon she was grazing steadily, her shadow long in the moonlight. Sandy went to bed.

In the morning, she wondered if it had happened. Queen Moon was undisturbed. The sun shone. But Sandy felt abandoned, sick. She got dressed and went down the field to see Queen Moon as she always did. The mare looked up and started to walk towards her. Sandy leaned over the gate and saw a piece of paper wedged in the latch. She pulled it out and smoothed it open. In scrawled pencil it said, 'I would like you to have Queen Moon for your own. You are the only person. See you. J.'

Sandy had to be alone. She went over the seawall and sat there, looking at the river in the early-morning sunshine until she had got her brain back in order. Then she floated home. She had missed the school bus.

'Where on earth have you been?' her mother asked.

'By the river.'

'Why are you smiling like that? You look as if you've found the end of the rainbow.'

It must have been infectious. Her mother was smiling too.

'Yes,' said Sandy.

THE END

ABOUT THE AUTHOR

'There are very few born story-tellers. K. M. Peyton is one of them.' THE TIMES

Kathleen Peyton's first book was published while she was still at school and since then she has written over thirty novels. She is probably best known for *Flambards* which, with its sequels *The Edge of the Cloud* and *Flambards in Summer*, was made into a 13-part serial by Yorkshire Television in 1979. *The Edge of the Cloud* won the Library Association's Carnegie Medal in 1969 and the *Flambards* trilogy won the *Guardian* Award in 1970. More recently, BBC TV televised her best-selling title *Who Sir? Me Sir?*

In addition to *The Boy Who Wasn't There*, Kathleen Peyton is the author of several other titles published by Transworld: *Darkling* (for young adult readers), *Poor Badger* (for younger readers) and, coming shortly in Doubleday hardcover, *The Swallow Tale*. She lives in Essex.